A. Hermann Bernard, Fr. Arnold

Legends of the Rhine

A. Hermann Bernard, Fr. Arnold

Legends of the Rhine

ISBN/EAN: 9783337384258

Printed in Europe, USA, Canada, Australia, Japan

Cover: Foto ©Andreas Hilbeck / pixelio.de

More available books at **www.hansebooks.com**

LEGENDS
OF THE RHINE,

by

A. H. Bernard.

———————

Translated from the German

by

Fr. Arnold,

Professor of languages.

Eight Edition.

MAYENCE,
by JOSEPH HALENZA.

Legends of the Rhine.

PREFACE.

The great celebrity which the German edition of this work has acquired in Germany, prompted me to publish it in the English language, not only for the purpose of attracting the attention of strangers to the most interesting traditions of the Rhine, but also as an entertainment for the tourist who visits the banks of this beautiful river.

I subjoin here an abridgement of a review of the work, which appeared in the year 1862 in the „Blätter für litterarische Unterhaltung" at Leipsic.

Prominent among the German literary novelties which appeared in the year 1862, is to be distinguished a „Collection of legends of the Rhine" by A. Hermann Bernard of Mayence. The autor has treated his subject with much taste and without losing any of its original simplicity. He chose the most popular traditions, amongst which are to be found many hitherto unknown, such as: „The noble lady of Schwanau": „Adolphseck and Imagina, the mistress of the emperor Adolphus of Nassau;" „The devil's-ladder at Lorch;" „The castellan of Hammerstein", etc. which whe have read with much pleasure. The historical traditions of this collection are very touching for instance: „Arnold of Walpoden at Mayence;" „The templars of Lahneck;" „The Cathedral of Cologne" etc.

Differing from the ordinary collections, this work of Bernard gives us also the tradition of the „Jewish colonists", whom Dahlberg, a Roman centurion and nobleman, brought to Worms, his native town, as his share of the booty after the destruction of Jerusalem; then he gives us the tradition of the prophetess „Jetta at Heidelberg", who is represented as a young girl of wonderful beauty, but who was visited with a terrible death by the Goddes Hertha for having fallen in love.

My only recommendation in offering

this work to the public is that it has
outlived seven editions within a short time
and I trust the readers of this, the eight,
will carry back with them pleasant remi-
niscences of scenes viewed, and hours
spent in places, herein described.

The publisher.

Strasburg.

In Strasburg there once lived a clock-maker who, through his masterly and clever works had attained a great reputation. He lived in perfect retirement and knew no higher pleasure, than his studies and the society of his beautiful young daughter, who since her mother's death managed his household.

All the thoughts and efforts of the master were aimed at producing still higher and better works of art; he began to brood, secluded himself and fell, in consequence, into tolerably bad repute with his neighbours. But when he at last began to neglect even the common duties of life and derange his household, he lost all reputation and if any body spoke of him, he was called a dreamer, too unpractical for life.

Every one thought — as is the custom — that he could apply to himself the famous saying of the Pharisees: „I thank God, that I am not as this man!"

1

Indeed the master himself, absorbed in his studies and ideas, cared little what his neighbours thought of him; he seldom went out, and if he did, he was too deeply absorbed in his meditations to notice things about him.

It was otherwise with his young daughter who with secret pain saw her dear father become gloomy. Her eyes were often seen in tears and her hands folded in prayer that the father might soon attain the end of his studies, diligent labours and speculations.

Among the few who visited the masters's house, two persons, who interested themselves in his fate, played a conspicuous part. The one was an elderly man with a slow gait, pointed features and mischivous eyes. He was rich and had after unspeakable pains finally attained the prospect of a magistracy. He already stood some time in connexion with the master and wooed the daugther; but she avcided him, for his attentions disgusted her.

The other, on the contrary, was a merry young fellow full of candour and honesty. He had devoted himself to the same art as the master and called upon him frequently, to converse with him about his works.

His greatest pleasure was to sit for hours near the maid and watch her working, and when he spoke of his art and of the end to be

attained, then his eyes sparkled, his cheeks
glowed and his breast heaved; the maid listened
with ecstasy to his words, often found herself
with her hands reposing and her eyes fixed with
inspiration on the young man.

Although neither had yet spoken of love, sympathy had filled their souls and revealed itself
to the impartial observer through most trifling
actions. Their hearts were innocent and they
comprehended not what they felt; timidity
chained their tongues and only the tender looks
of the young people betrayed the presence of
Cupid who but waited for an opportunity to
manifest himself.

Months passed in this manner, till one day
the candidate for the magistracy, sweetly smiling, approached the master and announced to
him his final advancement. He could not withstand subjoining to his speech a significant remark
upon his present power and he did it with all
the maliciousness which lurked at the bottom of
his soul. The master congratulated him heartily
and expressed the hope, that he would use his
power to the benefit and prosperity of the town
and his fellow-citizens.

„And now, dear friend and master!“ replied
the magistrate, permit me to utter a second wish
which like the first lies for a long time at the
bottom of my heart. You know, dear master,

that I am unmarried. Circumstances hindered me to think earlier of marriage, but now, having the title of magistrate, I think it my duty to reflect also upon this matter. You know me; I was always well meaning towards you, and your charming daughter seems especially fit, to secure my happiness and to render our connexion more solid and durable. I doubt not, as a magistrate, that I shall be welcome to you and therefore duly solicit your daughter's hand.

The master who had, during the long marriage proposal, found time to recover from his surprise, called his daughter without replying, to tell her what had happened.

Guta — this was the name of the maid — when she heard of the news grew pale and flew to the breast of her father.

„I shall return," continued the wooer, not appearing to notice the gestures of the maid: „reflect upon the matter, Miss; I can make you one of the most noble ladies of the town; I have the power to help your father and I would regret if you took a hasty resolution, which might harm you and your family. I leave you, with the hope of a favourable answer! Farewell!"

Saying this he bowed and retired, looking at the girl with a glance so mischievous and full of meaning, that she shuddered in her inmost heart and would have sunk down, if her maidenly pride had not supported her. But after his departure she lost her feigned strength and with a flood of tears sunk down, nearly fainting.

„Guta, my dear child, what ails you?“ asked the father, softly raising her head. „Do his advances frighten you? Speak freely, choose as you like and don't mind the menaces hidden in his words, for they will rebound powerless from my efforts. But few weeks“ — said he to himself „and I shall have finished my work; glory and wealth will then be mine and I may boldly compare myself with the richest and most esteemed citizens of our town!“

„Papa“, whispered Guta — „I can't marry him! I shudder only to think of it!“

„Then let us speak no more of it!“ He will understand and the matter is settled!“

But in this the master was wrong. The wooer, having heard Guta's refusal, boiled and foamed with rage and uttered menaces, which frightend the maid. „Indeed, you shall repent this! cried he, hastening away and nearly knocking the young man down, who had just entered the house.

The youth came just in time to calm the anxious girl. He listened with deep emotion to her report; his cheeks glowed with anger and he clenched his fist, when he heard of the threatenings which the disgusting man had uttered against her father. But when she at last, with a flood of tears, confessed to her lover her detestation of such a union, the expression of anger disappeared from his face and gave way to a feeling of tenderness.

Like a river breaking its dam, his constrained flood of love broke from his heart and flowed with ardour from his lips.

With ecstasy and hardly daring to breathe Guta heard the words of the youth resounding in her bosom. Grief and woe vanished and gave way to an unutterable feeling of happiness. What could she say to the young man when he asked, if his love was pleasing to her and what he might hope? Her lips were mute, but her tender and expressive looks told him enough as he pressed her with rapture to his breast.

In the excess of his joy he was about to hasten to her father, to claim her hand.

But Guta, half anxious, detained him saying:

„Don't go! — At least not now; for my father is deeply shocked by the last events; let us wait a few weeks more; he will then have finished his work and be more inclined, to hear of our love."

„Why", cried the youth with resolution, „then he shall at least accept me as his partner in business, that it may no longer suffer by his retirement. — Only let me! I will persuade him.

He loves me and will have no objection to my proposal."

So saying he left the maid, returning after a while glad and rejoicing; he communicated to the half anxious girl that her father had accepted him as a partner and granted him free management of his affairs.

„You see, Guta? I kann now take care of you. I shall be diligent, and if your father's plans don't succeed, his business will at least be secure!"

The happy lovers conversed much and for a long time, until they separated to commence their new life on the following day. — Weeks passed away in happiness and each day they had reason to congratulate themselves upon their new order of life. Guta, since the dearest object in her life was now entrusted to her care, had become more happy and blooming. The youth, as well as she, understood how to render their daily intercourse more pleasing and the father himself seemed animated by the calm happiness of the young people. The wrinkles disappeared from his face and with them the unpleasant and sickly irritability of his soul. A joyful, but calm serenity entered the house, before so gloomy under the before mentioned circumstances.

It was as if the sun's warm rays had penetrated a dark, unwholesome room and purified the atmosphere.

One day, while Guta was diligently employed with her work, which she now and then discontinued to look tenderly at her lover who was at work also, she suddenly heard her father uttering loud shouts of joy and soon after calling her by name.

Guta started with surprise and hastened to him; the assistant also rose and softly approached the door, through which she had disappeared.

Astonished and deeply moved, he stopped at the view, which presented itself to him. A boldly constructed clock-work moved lightly and easily in its springs at the same time giving an artificial life to several neat figures. Before it stood the master, his white locks in disorder, but his face proud and full of dignity. With a look of satisfaction he gazed at the movement of the wheels, while his arms entwined the graceful form of the young girl, who concealed her tears on his breast. Filled with reverence, the young man at last approached and silently pressed the hand offered to him by the master and scrutinizingly fixed his eyes on the work, which more and more excited his admiration. It was a great event when the master offered his work to the public view; his name was on every tongue and those who before had despised him, were now the first to approach and praise him the most.

Time, customs and manners may change, but the principles, which lie in the hearts of men and out of which the character, according to the education and cultivation, is developed, never.

For a long time the magistrate refused his approbation of this wonderful work, and regarded it — thanks to the insinuations of the discarded lover — as the idle productions of a fantastic brain.

But as soon as the master's fame spread abroad and members of the guild arrived from Basel to admire the work, the magistrate was compelled to enquire into the matter and grant him his approval.

Nay, when the citizens of Basel made efforts to put themselves in possession of the work, the corporation of Strasburg agreed to buy it and selected a side-chapel in the cathedral for its erection.

But the citizens of Basel, not satisfied with the issue of this affair, requested the master to construct a similar work for them and offered a considerable sum for its completion. Soon after the rumour of this reached the ears of the public, a great excitement seized them and thyel oudly opposed the proposal of the strangers. „What would become of the glory of our town, if other towns could triumph in an equal work of art?“ said they, and among them especially the offended wooer „The master must never be permitted to construct a second clock, it would be treason to the town; to prevent it, is our first duty."

In accordance with this opinion, the opponents of this clever man caused him to be brought before a tribunal, where his enemy sat as president.

The master was summoned before them, to promise never to build a second clock; but he firmly and proudly refused, saying: „God has given me talents and the power of being useful to my fellow-creatures; would it not therefore be cowardly and ungrateful, were I to accede to your request and not make use of the gifts with which He has endowed me! When I worked and studied day and night, you turned away from me and derided me as a foolish dreamer and only now, when the citizens of Basel have praised me, have you come to criticise my work. Love for my native town has induced me to yield the work to you rather than to others. I have now done enough for my town and its glory and see no crime in benefitting others by my art."

Clad in his simple dress, his form drawn to its full height, he proudly stood before the glittering array of counsellors, who were compelled to cast down their eyes before his noble and manly look. But after he was led away and the president could again give vent to his hatred, the assembly assented to his proposal of blinding the master. „For" they argued „only in this manner can we make certain, that he will never construct a second clock." With a painful smile at the blindness and perverseness of his fellow-citizens, the accused man heard the dreadful sentence. He neither uttered a cry of terror, nor of fear; his manner only expressed contempt and pity. He was asked, if he wished anything before the execution of the sentence. After reflecting some time, he expressed the desire that he might undergo his punishment in the presence of his work and also be permitted to give it some final improvements.

His request was granted. Long and tenderly the old man gazed at his clock. But his enemy, stimulated by revenge and the desire to see his victim soon miserable, reminded him of the fleeting time and did not omit to compare the past with the present.

Rage seized the master at being thus taunted. By some skilful movement of the work he took out the clock; having done so, he willingly surrendered himself to the hands of his executioners In the clock it suddenly began to whirr, and discordant sounds came therefrom which mingled with the scornful laugther of the tortured man. The weights fell to the ground; the bell struck disharmoniously 13-times and breathed out its last sounds like the sigh of a dying man. The master stood with his form erect like a demon of revenge and cried: „Now rejoice, in my work, proud citizens; the clock is destroyed and my revenge complete!“ All who stood around were seized with horror and consternation at the sight; the assistant approached and softly led the old man into the arms of his disconsolate daughter.

After the first excitement of feeling was over, they deliberated upon the course of life now to be pursued. The lovers had confessed their attachment without reserve and received the paternal blessing. The old man was consoled for the lost glory of his work by the happiness and contentment which dwelt in their little circle. The wretched man who incited the town to commit the dreadful crime, was forfeited to the general contempt and died expelled and cursed by all who uttered his name.

The clock remained destroyed till the year 1842, when the trial in restoring it at last succeeded.

The glory of the restorer is now associated with that of the constructor.

Schwanau.

In the forteenth century there existed between the citizens of Strasburg and the knight Walter of Schwanau a feud, the last named having several times inflicted considerable loss on the merchants of Strasburg through having waylaid and robbed them.

In those times the citizens were obliged to defend themselves and maintain a sufficient number of soldiers, to keep the knights in awe. — But as the knights could often levy a considerable army, the citizens of one town were obliged to band themselves with other towns.

Walter was one of those knights, who trusting in his numerous forces could without fear commence a war with a town like Strasburg and even when he heard that his enemies had made an alliance with several Swiss towns against him he laughed at the idea; for he knew the manner in which the towns and their represen-tatives managed that, after having spent years in deliberating, they only arrived at the conclusion that something ought to be done.

But above all, his castle was strong, situated on an inaccesable rock, well provided with provisions and manned with fellows as bold as himself, most of whom were outlaws. He never dreamt of a blockade and if an assault were attempted, there was no doubt that the enemy would be repelled with gread loss.

This time however the citizens had quickly and prudently determined to commence war, and confided the command of the army to an old and experienced colonel, who instead of assailing the castle surrounded it, with the intention of starving out the garrison.

Walter seeing himself thus outwitted, began to fear for the consequences, and felt inclined to commence a negotiation, which he, in the beginning had scornfully refused. His soldiers, who at last, when the provisions were in the decline, began to murmur, advised him to send a messenger with negotiations to the colonel. But as the enemy's messengers, who summoned Walter to surrender, had been repulsed with scorn — so was his messenger now treated with contempt, even before he had spoken to the colonel.

Walter heard the news with grief and rage; a deep melancholy settled upon his brow, for he foresaw the ruin of himself and his wife, whom he loved truly and tenderly. Since the beginning of the war the noble lady had lived in constant anxiety and trouble, which was now increased by the sadness which her husband could no longer conceal; she pressed him with words of love and kindness, till he at length acknowledged the critical position he was in, and the insult that had been offered to his messenger. A sudden thought, crossed her mind, resolution glowed in her bosom and beamed from her eyes. „If every hope is lost“, said she, „there is yet one thing remaining; that is for me to treat with the enemy, Do not fear that I will humble myself“ added she quickly, perceiving the refusing gesture of her husband. „I know what I owe to ourselves and our name; they will not dare to insult a woman. The colonel must listen to me, he will see that it is better to attain his aim in an amicable manner, than to drive us to desperation. Believe me, he will be prudent and reflect wisely upon it; he will curb his hatred and prefer certainty to risking his honour in a doubtful combat.“ —

Walter tried to speak, but she stopped his words with kisses, and begged so long, that he at length unwillingly consented. The lady lost no time in putting her plan into execution. She feared her husband would withdraw his consent. She therefore took her little son upon her arm and walked to the camp, having previously prayed for help and protection.

The colonel received the lady, who was clad in mourning, coldly but politely. He could not however remain long insensible to her words which flowed like the warm breath of spring from her lips, and melted his icy heart. He was displeased with himself at being moved and feigned an anger which he did not feel: he however granted the lady a retreat with all her treasures.

„Well then, replied the lady, „take possession of the castle in peace for my husband is saved, — he and my child are my treasures, all else are trifles which I willingly abandon. Trusting in your word I will depart with these, and fervently pray to heaven, that you may be rewarded. I know my husband has grievously offended the citizens and that they desire his capture, to revenge themselves on him who had injured them so much. On my husband only can their revenge fall, he being the chief, and now you have granted him free retreat you will not revenge yourselves on his followers, for the faults he committed. Take the castle then, for I go forth with my treasures — but be merciful to the others!"

Surprise and compassion were to be alternately seen in the face of the old warrior; at lenght pity prevailed and when the lady ceased to speak, the colonel turned aside to conceal his emotion. He then approached the lady; kindly offered her his hand and kissing her little son said:

„You have triumphed, noble lady and your husband is saved through you! But take your other treasures with you also — far be it from me, not to honour fidelity so noble and generous as yours. The castle however must be destroyed, but I will do all in my power for the soldiers.“

And so it happened. The knight went forth with his wife, child, and treasures; his soldiers, for the most part, entered the army of the confederate towns, but the castle was destroyed.

Staufenberg.

eter, lord of Staufenberg, once lost his way when hunting and arrived extremely tired and nearly fainting at a spring situated in a deep forest. The water flowed beneath the riche foliage of luxurious herbs, while a soft bottom of fragrant moss covered the ground around. The youth highly rejoiced at finding such a charming and shadowy haunt quite appropriate for the flight of his imaginations approached the spring and moistened his lips with its crystal fluid; he then walked along the brook, to seek its source.

He was suddenly and agreeably surprised to find a lovely girl sitting under a stately oak wringing out her wet hair and braiding it.

The youth, almost confused by the charming view, stopped and scarcely dared to breathe. His heart beat audibly and his looks were fixed on the charms of the forest-child who, with innocence, displayed its feet and bosom to his gaze.

Staufenberg.

At last Peter recovered his manly spirit and stepped softly forward, for he was anxious to know, who she was and why she lived thus in the solitude of the woods. The noise of his steps alarmed the maid. She looked up and a charming blush spread over her face and bosom when she perceived the youth with his eyes steadfastly fixed upon her.

With stuttering voice he asked her if she would permit him to rest near her. She assented and, as she blushingly drew her rich tresses over her form and hid her small feet in her gown, appeared to him a being worthy of adoration.

He stretched himself near her on the soft moss, leaned his head upon his hand and became absorbed in the contemplation of her. The increasing embarassment of the maid caused her to appear more beautiful, so that the heart of the young man became still more inflamed with love.

He was finally roused from his reverie by her look, in which was mingled love, reproach and bashfulness.

The youth felt the unbecomingness of his staring and sighed loudly like one, who awakes from a dream.

„Forgive me, dear girl, if I have admired your lovely face too long and attentively; a strange and charming dream filled my heart; it

2*

seemed to me, as if I were the only happy being permitted to view your beautiful face. Allow me to make amends for my neglect and before all receive my thanks for having allowed me to rest near you."

„Not so, noble Sir!" replied the maid kindly: „you are the lord of this ground and I must thank your for having allowed me, to remain here."

„Oh, that I could render this place a paradise, that you might never wish to leave it! Since I saw you it has become a paradise for me," added he with a tender expression of his eyes. „Oh, don't turn away, sweet maid; forgive me, if I can no longer conceal my violent feelings. I love you with ardour and would be the happiest of men if you would accept me as your husband and become the lady of my castle and these grounds."

The youth, who, after having confessed his love in a passionate flow of words now took the hand of the maiden and covered it with kisses, at the same time, with eager entreaties and kind words, begged her to consent to his proposal.

„O speak!" exclaimed he. „Dare I hope or must I fear! Can you love me! Disperse the doubts, which render me unhappy."

„I love you," whispered she tenderly, bending her rosy little face towards him and resting her looks on the happy youth. „I have loved you longer than you imagine!"

„Then you consent, to be my wife?"

„I dare not tell you to day; come again to morrow at the same hour, but leave me now, for my time is over!"

„Then you will be here and I shall see you again?"

He rose quickly, embraced the blushing maid and imprinting a burning kiss on her lips rushed off, for he feared by a longer stay to lose his self possession and not obey her.

On the next day, at the same hour, he returned to the spring, where he found his beloved adorned with a fragrant wreath of may flowers.

With sweet smiles and looks of love she offered him her pretty little hand and invited him to sit by her side.

She then informed him, that she was a water-nymph and goddess of that spring, that she had loved him for a long-time and would esteem it as the highest bliss, to be mistress of his affections.

„And if you still wish, noble sir, to make me your wife, I will follow you every-where, only," — and when she said this, a melancholy expression covered her face, „only you must be faithful to me, for infidelity would bring death to you and eternal woe to me!"

„Faithful until death! cried the youth passion-
atly, pressing her to his heart and covering her
lips and eyes with burning kisses. „Never shall
another maid conquer the heart, that is devoted
to you and which will be eternally yours!

The mariage-ceremony was celebrated silently,
and without pomp or splendour. True happiness
requires no outward show which is often used,
to conceal the woe of the heart. The young
pair were happy in each others love; the world
had no cares for them, their life was a heaven.
They seemed to gain in youth and their love for
each other day by day to increase.

When in course of time a lovely boy became
the fruit of their union, their joy knew no bounds
and the young couple felt their attachment and
love had thereby become more firm. The higher
the happiness, the nearer the woe!

The report spread like lightning that war
had broken out in France and many nobles and
knights of Germany, allured by gain and glory
partook in it.

Peter also heard the news and ambition, like
a sad summoner stirred his soul and seemed to
reproach him for allowing the sword of his ancestors to rust in its scabbard, while other knights
gained glory by their valiant deeds. He became
restless, his mind was tormented and distracted;

even the caresses of his young wife had not the same charm for him as formerly.

With silent grief she perceived, that the mind of her beloved husband was not content with domestic happiness and that his thoughts were centered in the seat of war. The knight did his utmost to conceal his longing, but could not help betraying himself in unguarded moments, which encouraged his wife to carry out the plan which she had formed. She presented him one day with a splendid belt, which she had worked and begged him, to wear it in battle as a token of her love.

„I know,“ said she. „You long to depart for France, to wield the sword of your ancestors in battle. Although it grieves me to part from you, I agree nevertheless, that you shall satisfy your burning desire, which, I fear, will destroy our happiness. — Go, dear husband; gain laurels and glory by valiant deeds, but return and then learn, that the happiness, which you enjoy at my side, is far better, than that, to be found amongst strangers.“

The knight, touched by her generosity and devotion pressed her to his bosom and kissed the tears from her cheeks.

„Thanks, thanks!“ exclaimed he, „embracing her repeatedly, you read my soul and seem to know, how the desire to do honour to the name of my ancestors and our rank burns within me. It calls me to battle, and my arms seem to reproach me for lingering; I accept therefore your belt as a sign of luck; for my beloved gave it and it will guide me back to her."

Leaning on his breast, she conducted him to the childs cradle and offered him his lips for a parting kiss. "He shall be my consolation in your absence!" sobbed she. "And think often of us!"

"Always, always!" swore the knight, "whose eyes were bathed in tears. I shall never forget you and our child!"

"Then go, but return as soon as possible! I shall stand at the window every evening and anxiously wait for you. Don't forget your promise and remember my warning before I became your wife.

With tender kisses the knight sealed his vows of fidelity anew and then began to prepare for his depature, wherein his wife calmly and prudently aided him. It was, as if invisible hands carried all things requisite together; so quickly and noiselessly, the packing was carried on.

It was only at his depature that Peter became aware of the great blessing that a quiet careful, loving wife was. Had not passionate ambition blinded him, he would have remained in his castle and enjoyed the pure happiness the company of such a wife afforded; but after a

long leave-taking from her, he departed with
full speed for an unknown country, where his
fancy showed him brilliant images of glory,
splendour and battles. Before him he saw the
future; if he looked back from his steed, he perceived his wife, waving him a farewell, thereby
driving all thoughts of the dangers of war from
his mind.

At last the forest hid the castle from his
view; he then put spurs to his steed crying,
„Onward, soldiers; before us lies glory, behind
us love; the sooner we gain the first, the sooner
we shall enjoy the pleasures of the last!"

And „Onward" echoed from his bearded followers who spurred their horses as they galloped
madly forward.

Peter immediately after his arrival in France
placed himself and his troop at the disposal of
a duke of that country and distinguished himself
by his valour and prudence so much that the
duke was anxious to attach this valiant and
honest warrior permanently to his cause.

But what to offer him as an inducement to
exchange his freedom for a vassalage had puzz-
led the Duke for some time, when one day he
perceived his youngest daughter looking at the
handsome young knight with glances more tender and affectionate than she was wont to do
at the other knights. The duke saw, that a union

between his daughter and Peter would be the easiest way of realizing his wish and therefore offered, as a reward for his services, the hand of the maid whose youth, beauty and noble rank rendered her worthy of the highest in the land.

The knight, whose simple mind was already dazzled by the splendour of the Franconian court, accepted the offer with a feeling of satisfied vanity. It flattered him, to be chosen as the husband of a young, beautiful princess; dazzled by the glitter of the crown which she wore, and by the splendour of the court, he entirely forgot the promise given to his chaste and lovely wife. He surrendered himself to the intoxicating sound of pleasures which the duke prepared for him and did not resist or reflect upon the changes which his heart had undergone. It was only at night when the eye was not dazzled by the view of the brilliant festivities that, a pale figure arose in his mind and looked at him in silence and sorrow. Although he as often tried to banish this vision and avoid the expressive looks of his grievously injured wife, he failed. Her eyes followed him with looks more of reproach than anger. He became unsetted and disconten-ted. He remembered his beautiful wife, his pretty little boy and the happy peaceful days which he had passed in his castle; he compared all this with the restless life of the court and insa-

tiable desire for its gaiety and began to realize
the fact that his castle contained a higher treasure than a crown, even on the head of the
most beautiful maiden. He formed the best resolutions, vowing to return home, and to fly from
the seductions of the court; but at daybreak the
images of the night vanished before the brightness of the sun; shame prevented him taking
his leave and he felt himself attracted anew by
the charms of his lovely bride.

Weeks thus passed away in painful struggles
with his heart; he became melancholy and dejected and could not, even when at the side of the
princess, banish his grief. He at last resolved,
to ask the advice of a priest and communicate
his sorrows to him.

A priest whose plump and ruddy countenance
shone brightly, listened with astonishment to the
knight's tale, at the conclusion of which his
cheeks grew paler and he exclaimed with fear,
at the same time crossing himself thrice.

„You have made an alliance with the devil;
Angels and heavenly spirits don't beget children
with men; that is only the case with infernal
beings, wo do so to spread their power. Your
soul is forfeited to the devil and I consider it
my duty, if you don't abjure the union with that
being and do penance, to withhold the benefits
of the church from you."

The knight half terrified, half rejoiced by the priest's words, clung with desperate ardour to the idea, that his wife was an unholy being, to whom it was a sin to be united.

Half persuaded, half infatuated he consented to abjure her, unterwent penances and the duke, in agreement with the priest, fixed the day, on which the knight should be entirely free'd from the bonds of Satan, by marrying him to the princess.

As the marriage-day approached, the embarassment of the knight grew more painful. Like a night-mare his mind was worked upon and the looks of his abjured wife appeared to him in his dreams more and more sorrowful.

Pale and with hair erect the knight arose from his couch at the dawn of the wedding-day and hastened to the window, where the suns rays shone warmly upon him. The bells rang merrily as the servants entered, to dress their master.

With a vacant stare and like one in a trance he allowed them do with him as they pleased. He then mounted his horse and rode, followed by a stately and splendid train of knights, towards her castle without noticing the astonished looks of the girls and women, who had assembled to see him pass.

The bride in her splendid wedding-dress, received him and bearing on her head a coronet from which a long, fragrant veil descended to the ground. But her smiles had no charms for him and when he bent down, to kiss her hand, it seemed to him like the hand of a corpse; terror stricken and with a ghastly look he staggered back.

The marriage-procession moved on; it was obliged to pass over a bridge, beneath which a stream rolled calmy. Dark clouds suddenly covered the sky and announced the approach of a thunderstorm; as the bridegroom stepped on the bridge, a flash of lightning glanced before him. The storm raged wildly and the torrent rose to his horses hoofs. The animal plunged and reared through fear: „My dream!" exclaimed Peter, — whose face had now became deathly pale and contrasted frightfully with his wedding dress — and fiercely spurring his horse sprang into the foaming waters.

The storm abated, the sun shone forth and the stream rolled under the bridge whereon the trembling bride and her attendants still stood.

It was at the same time that a fierce storm accompanied by thunder and lightning raged over Staufenberg and when it had ceased, the lady of the castle with her child could not be found. Nobody knew whither she had gone; but at midnight loud weeping was heard accompanied by the whimpering of a child and from the tops of the fir-trees a voice seemed to whisper „Woe to faithless men!"

The „Klingelkapelle".

Shortly after the introduction of Christianity into Germany, a hermit took possession of a deserted cell near Gernsbach (on the way between Gernsbach and the castle of Eberstein) who besides his contemplative life, preached the gospel to the inhabitants of that part of the country.

One evening as a storm raged, the wind groaned and whistled through the tops of the oak and fir-trees, and the rain poured, he heard a soft supplicant voice, outside begging for shelter and protection.

The hermit looked out and saw a beautiful young female before his cell, who, shivering with cold tried to wrap herself in the few garments which scantily clung around her form.

„Let me in", begged she „to warm myself at your fire, for I am weary and cold."

The hermit willingly complied, offered her honey and wine and bade her sit down at his fire-side.

After she had refreshed herself, the hermit began by asking her whence she came and what had driven her out in such a stormy night.

„A vow!“ replied the maid. „Persecuted and despised I was obliged to leave a pleasant and endeared cell, which I inhabited; I will return thiter and dig my tomb in it.“

„Then you are a female-hermit not with standing that you are so young and pretty. I would rather have deemed you a child, than a woman!“

With these words the hermit neared the girl and fixed his looks upon her, whose beauty seemed to strike him.

„Yes like you, I am also wont to live in the forest and worship my Gods; I was devoted to the service of Hertha, but you Christians, who preach love and exercise intolerance expelled me from my cell and drove me out in the night. Woe, woe to you! Hertha will revenge me!“

„Then you are not a Christian?“ said the monk terrified and unvoluntarily starting back from the heathen-maid who calmly sat near the fire, and with the point of a little staff traced runic letters on the ground.

„You are frightened because I am no Christian? Am I not as young and beautiful as you? Am I not flesh and blood like you? Look! This is the cell which once belonged to me and now I am obliged to beg shelter in it; my hand planted this moss and I myself worked this decoration to the honour of Hertha. — Does this cell shelter you less because it once belonged to me? Do you sleep less softly on this couch, or look with less pleasure on this decoration because it is my work? Look at the stars and admire the brightness and immensity of the heaven! Is there not room enough for your God and mine? Why do you persecute me?

„Stop, unfortunate maid! You are sinning against one who preached love to mankind and died on the cross for our sins. There is greater joy in heaven for one converted, than for a hundred righteous, and God has led you to my cell, that I may deliver your soul from eternal damnation!"

After these words and a fervent prayer he turned again to the maid and spoke to her of the life, passion and death of our Saviour.

But his heart felt not, what he spoke, for the beauty of the maid dazzled his senses and unsettled his mind.

And when she appeared to attend to his words and approach nearer to him, when her breath touched his cheek and she drew his hand to her bosom, his blood ran, like glowing fire, through his veins and the words died upon his lips.

The maid, conscious of her power, failed not to ensnare him more and more, with her seemingly

3

innocent and childish behaviour and when she thought him entirely in her power she desired him to break the cross, before which he was wont to pray.

She expressed the wish with such a charming ingenuousness and fascination, that the monk vanquished at last and was about to consent to her desire. He had already stretched out his hand towards the cross, but a that moment a bell outside rang, the sound of which stirred his consciense. Repentant and ashamed he knelt down and prayed. When he rose, the apparition had dissappeared.

The little bell, which un invisible hand had fastened to a bough and rung, was carried by the hermit into his cell, as a warning of his weakness and from this time the place, was called the „Klingelcapelle“ (tinkling-chapel).

The Mermaid.

One evening as the lasses and lads of Seebach were assembled in the spinning-room, the former, for the purpose of twisting the linen thread, of which the dress of those times chiefly consisted, and the latter, for the purpose of amusing the lasses with jokes, tales or harmless sports, a lovely young lady entered the room with a pretty spinning wheel made of ivory and modestly begged to be admitted into their company.

The young people were astonished by the appearance of the charming stranger, whom they had never seen before, but with obliging willingness consented, they drew their little circle together and the son of the house immediately brought, from the best room a chair, which evidently had been little used and was much finer than all the others. The assembly intimidated at first by the presence of the stranger, by degrees regained their former spirits. They joked, laughed and

3*

sang and when the strange lady at last departed, all praised her mightily and discussed strange and imaginary tales of her origin and residence.

The majority were of the opinon that she must be one of the mermaids of the Mummellake, which spreads its dark waters under the mountain to an unfathomable depth. The only one, who had not given his opinin upon the maiden and had been silent since her arrival and particularly so since her departure was the son of the house. He was a fine, modest youth and more educated than his comrades, his father was the richest man of the country and wished to make him a person of distinction, as for instance, a councillor or magistrate; to tell the truth, his ideas on that point were still very vague.

The lady returned precisely at the same hour as the day before and after a cordial greeting calmly sat down in her place and began to spin. The son of the house sat opposite her in a corner of the room in silence. When the soft and pleasing looks of the young lady rested upon him and she favoured him with a nod his cheeks would glow and he felt, as if a warm hand had touched his heart.

The lady departed exactly at the same hour as the previous day and appeared regularly every evening in the merry circle, but she always kept the same hour of departure and no entreaties could persuade her, to stay longer.

Since she frequented the spinning-room, the lasses were by far more diligent than before, their spinning was much finer and their distaffs better filled.

Besides this they also became more cheerful and if the saying of the lads be true, much neater and more tasteful in their dress. It seemed as if a ray of brightness issued from the stranger, ennobling and embellishing every thing around her.

All were accustomed to the appearance of the lady and waited anxiously for the hour of her arrival. The happiest of them all was then the son of the house to whom the hours of her absence were a blank in his existence. During her absence he grew pale and only at her return his features wore a lively aspect.

One evening he determined to turn the hands of the clock back, so as to enjoy the presence of the young lady longer. He carried out his plan and when the hour of the lady's departure arrived, he slunk silently away for the purpose of following her.

The lady seemed to have divined the irregularity, for at the striking of the clock she hastily bade farewell and hurried away in the direction of the lake.

The youth followed her, saw her plunge into the water and soon after heard a low whining, after which the lake boiled and foamed.

Excited and fearing mischief he sprang after her, but by a miraculous power he was drawn into the depths and disappeared.

The next day some wood-cutters found his corpse in the lake near which blood and some bunches of woman's-hair were floating. The „Lady of the lake" was never seen again.

———

Yburg.

arious traditions are connected with the ruins of the castle of Yburg, and indeed these ruins seem to impress one with ghost-stories and their concomitant spectres and goblins.

At one time Gustav Wasa's grandson established his alchymical laboratory there in which he, in connexion with Pestalozzi exercised his magic art. At annother time the monks of Baden tied up all the ghosts and goblins which haunted that neighbourhood, in a bag and carried them to Yburg, — certainly a very ingenious proceeding and which can only be accounted for by the choice of this wild spot for their abode.

It is said that the last of the race that built the castle, was a wild, dissipated fellow, who mortgaged his property and fell in consequence in great pecuniary distress. His creditors more than his conscience kept him in a perpetual state of anxiety.

One night after one of those scenes usual
with creditors, where threats, maledictions and
lamentation are not wanting, the knight dreamt,
he had discovered an inexhaustible treasure in
the sepulchral vaults of his ancestors. The next
day he descended into them, broke open the
coffins and not having found, what he had seen
in his dream, he uttered frightful execrations
against the avarice of his forefathers.

Just in the height of his fury, a horrible
figure with hideous laugther rose from out of
the ground and seemed to expand to the roof
almost suffocating the terrified knight.

Shaking with fear he knelt down, invoking God
and all the Saints, to assist him. He promised
to do penance and finish his life as a hermit.

Immediately after having made this vow, he
heard the voice of a child resounding from one
of the open coffins, revoking the spirit and ad-
monishing the knight to think of his salvation
as his days were numbered.

Amid peals of thunder and terrible noises the
demon vanished who in his flight cast a flash
of lightning upon the castle which split one of
the towers from top to bottom.

But the knight did, as he had vowed and it
may be hoped, that he paid his debts to heaven
more punctually, than those which he contracted
on earth.

Windeck.

I.

bout eight miles from Baden stands the castle of Windeck, which is haunted by the spirit of a girl who appears from time to time.

A young sportsman, whom the chase once led to the castle, saw the girl, who offered the tired hunter a goblet of most delicious wine. He was so charmed with her lovely appearance that he returned every day, in the hope of seeing the girl again.

But when he found, that all his endeavours were in vain and that he was obliged to return each time without having gained the object of his search he became melancholy and visibly pined away.

He at length made the castle his constant abode, where he led a quiet dreamy sort of life and was soon called by the peasants in the neighbourhood the „lord of the castle.“

One morning he was found dead, but with such a happy expression of features that every one was of opinion, that he had seen the maid of the castle.

Some added, her kiss had killed him. But when the people perceived a small ring on his finger, which they had never seen before, their opinion turned to conviction and they buried him with pious awe in the vault of the castle by the side of his ghostly bride.

II.

Near the above mentioned castle are still to be seen the vestiges of a deep ditch, called the „Hennegraben“, from which the neighbouring farm took its name.

It is said of the origin of this ditch, that the young relations of a dean of Strasburg, whom the knight of Windeck had imprisoned, came to beg for the release of their uncle. Arrived in the district of the castle, they met an old woman in the forest, who kindly asked them, what was the aim of their journey.

„We are going to the castle of Windeck!“ began the elder of the travellers, a slender, delicate youth: „Our uncle, the dean of Strasburg is imprisoned there and we are going to surrender ourselves as hostages, till he has paid his ransom.

„Ah! ah! Do you expect, that the lord of Windeck will accept you in his stead as hostages? And then how will such delicate, tendor boys be able to suffer the captivity, which threatens you in the castle? Heh?"

After saying which the old woman with cunning eyes examined the tender figure of the elder youth, who could scarce now suppres his tears.

„God will help us, for our uncle is our only support!" replied he softly, upon which his younger brother with childish candour, began by saying that he would challenge the knight. „Indeed, that I will!" added the boy seriously, „for I am a knight like him and I will deliver my uncle!"

„Hush, Cuno; don't speak, like a child, we must entreat and not defy!" said the edler brother.

„Eh what, Imma; you may beg, but I shall not!" replied the boy thereby bringing his disguised sister into the most painful embarassment and causing the blood to mount to her cheeks.

„You need not blush, maid!" continued the old woman, — „I remarked at the first glance, that you are a girl in disguise and I am inclined, to help you; for you are honest and I like you. — Go to the castle and tell the knight, that I sent you for the purpose of communicating to him, that the citizens of Strasburg have resolved to take his castle by surprise; he must cut a trench across the only possible ascent and as the time presses, I will give you something, that will enable the knight to open the ditch."

Saying this, she whistled a strange tune, upon which a grey hen flew upon the old woman's shoulder.

„Here, take it and bring it safe into the castle. When it grows dark and the moon rises carry it to the place and leave the remainder to us!"

The children looked at each other in astonishment. The old woman, after having spoken something in a strange dialect to the hen, gave it them, wished them goodbye, and reminded them at parting, to take care of the hen and do as she had bid them.

The disguised maiden and her brother travelled to the castle and were instantly presented to the knight, a fine young man, who received them with kindness.

The girl, with hesitation and embarrasment, could scarcely find words, to ask her request and deliver the message.

Regaining her self possesion at last she gave the knight the hen, at the same time begging him, to keep her and her brother as hostages instead of their imprisoned uncle.

A strange feeling overcame the knight, when he heard the proposition. And when the boy with childlike simplicity touched and admired the belt and accoutrements of the knight and expressed his delight with its splendour he took him in his arms and bade the elder youth follow.

Angry and dejected at the idea of being in the power of his enemy the dean sat brooding in a dark room. He walked impatiently up and down his small apartment and through a small grated window, looked at the distant country with longing glances.

After having given vent to his anger in execrations he sunk down upon his arm-chair and taking one of his books devoted himself to study, for he enjoyed, though imprisoned, every comfort, which he could wish, excepting his liberty.

The knight led the two boys to his cell and the heart of the elder beat anxiously under his doublet, when they stood before the door, which concealed their uncle. Scarce was the door opened, when the younger boy began to clap his hands joyously and cry:

„Uncle, uncle, Imma und I have come, to deliver you!“

The knight looked with astonishment at the blushing maid, whose sex was so suddenly announced. He did not betray himself and offered his hand with cordiality to the likewise astonished dean, saying:

„Did you hear that, dean? You are free, if you promise a ransom; yield these children to me as hostages, and I promise not to give them back so soon. Now young man“, said he jestingly to the embarrassed maid, „will you enter my service as a soldier or would you prefer a place in my household? You seem indeed much more fit for the latter, than for the former!“

But when the maiden looked at him with a timid and reproachful glance he could master himself no longer and pressed her to his breast, asking, if she would remain with him, instead of returning to her uncle.

He must have read a favourable answer in her looks and from her tears which she shed while leaning on his bosom, for he cheerfully summoned the dean, to change his prison-dress for the surplice and give them his blessing.

The dean at first did not seem inclined, to consent to the marriage; but when Imma too begged his consent, he mastered his anger and gave them his blessing.

The hen was placed where the old woman had indicated and on the following day, when the citizens of Strasburg approached, they found the newly made trench filled with the soldiers of Windeck and instead of a war-meeting they were invited to a wedding-dance.

———

Triefels.

ear Annweiler, upon one of the peaks
of the long chain of the Haardt-moun-
tains is situated the castle of Triefels,
in which Richard Coeur de Lion was
imprisoned.

One fine summer-morning a troop of horsemen passed through the county of the Haardt,
enlivening their journey with jests and merry
tales.

At their head rode three men; evidently the
leaders of the troop. They were noble figures,
whose appearance spoke of war and who seemed
to prefer the saddle and hardships to a life of ease.

After a close scrutiny it became apparent
that the centre one of the three was not a warrior; his looks and manners bespoke him to be
a man of thought and poetic feeling. In truth
such he turned out to be for he was no other
than the troubadour who had left his country to
seek his friend and king whose protracted absence
from his land caused great anxiety.

One of the knights had just finished a merry tale, which had excited the laughter of the whole troop, when the minstrel suddenly stopped his horse and listened with deep emotion to the plaintive and melancholy song of a young shepherd.

As soon as the song was finished, he spurred his horse towards the place, whence the voice came.

„My lad," cried he, „sing your song once more and I will give you this piece of gold!"

„With pleasure, Sir!" replied the shepherd politely, „it is a nice song and I like to sing it."

Having said this, he recommenced the strophe again and when he arrived at the last lines the voice of the knight mingled harmoniously with the boy's.

„Now tell me, lad, who thaught you this pleasant song?"

„It might be better not to tell!" replied the boy casting a suspicious glance at the knight.

„I will give you another piece of gold and my promise, that no harm shall be done you, if you tell!"

The lad, dazzled by the glittering piece of gold, timidly approached the knight and having previously looked round, said, that he had heard it sung in the castle of Triefels. where he sometimes kept watch over his sheep.

„Oh God!" exclaimed the knight with tears

4

in his eyes. „How wondrous are thy ways!“ taking off his helmet and with eyes upcast he fervently offered up a prayer.

His companions, with astonishment, surprised him in this attitude; but before they could question him, the mistrel turned towards them with sparkling eyes and said: „Found my lords! Onward to Triefels!“

The enthusiasm of the minstrel instantly seized the whole troop and they all repeated the cry: „Onward to Triefels!“

With hasty words the minstrel now communicated his discovery to his companions in a language unintelligible to the boy and when he had finished, all eyes sparkled with unutterable joy and every one bared his head, looking thankfully to heaven.

After the first excitement had subsided, they deliberated and agreed to take a view of the fortress first, in which the young shepherd could serve them as a guide. A handful of gold-coins rendered him compliant and the knights rode merrily towards Triefels.

On the way the shepherd, said, that the fortress was well guarded and that a stranger rarely crossed its draw-bridge. „I advise you, not to enter“, added he seriously, for the keeper is a peevish fellow and will not open the gate to you because you are in such great numbers.

„Quite right, boy; go on, we only intend to look at the castle and you can surely show us a place, where we can take up our lodgings.“

„Certainly I can, good sirs, for I know every house and cottage hereabout.“

With such and similar discourses they marched on, till they at last came in sight of Triefels, whose pinnacles were now gilded by the setting sun.

At the sight of Triefels the knights stopped and began to deliberate again.

„I think it better, my friends, if I exchange my military dress for a minstrel's tunic and in that manner try to get an entrance into the castle, if, as I hope he is, our noble king is imprisoned there, his friend's eye will surely detect him and find means for his deliverance; but you must remain in the neighbourhood of the castle so as, to be able to help me if I require your assistance.

So saying he left the troop and rode, followed by his servant, who bore his harp, up the hill, which led to the castle.

The shepherd was quite right in what he had said, regarding the castle; for the minstrel's reception was very ungracious. But one thing the shepherd had not mentioned and which consoled the stranger for his unpleasant reception namely the presence of the keeper's beautiful

4*

and amiable niece, who in that castle might well have been compared to a warm sun-ray in winter-time.

She persuaded her uncle, to grant the stranger a lodging and even prevailed upon the old man, to lend his ear to the songs of the minstrel. Thanks to his drowsy disposition he soon fell asleep and left the minstrel for some time alone with the maid, whose embarrassment by this pleasant „tête à tête“ became very perceptible, but it was not of long duration, as she shortly afterwards became as lively and cheerful as before.

„You seem very fond of music, miss,“ began the stranger, but I should think, that you find little opportunity of hearing it in this castle!

„You are right, indeed!“ replied the maid with a deep sigh, „I and a poor prisoner are the only ones in the castle, who sing and we both are but amateurs!“

„What did you say? A prisoner?“

„Yes, a prisoner! He must be of noble birth; but I dare not say more, for my uncle might hear it and would surely be angry, if I talked about him.

„Oh, dear maid, tell me but one thing,“ begged the stranger, speaking lowly and bending towards the maid:

„Were it possible for me to hear him? I should dearly like to hear a prisoner sing who sings for his freedom!"

„Then listen to night, for I regularly hear his melancholy plaint, which brings the tears to my eyes!"

„Oh! dear, good girl," cried the stranger, drawing her hand passionately to his lips; but suddenly recalled to himself, he let it fall and looked as much confused, as the young lady, whose bosom heaved with strange feelings.

Luckily for both, the old man at that moment awoke; after a short conversation he departed, having given orders, to lead the stranger to his apartment.

The latter entered his chamber with deep emotion, being so near his king and not knowing, how to save him. Silent and deeply musing he leaned on the window-seat, looking through the darkness and trying to find the tower, where he supposed his imprisoned friend to be.

He had been some time in this attitude when suddenly he heard an expressive, melancholy voice, singing the following strophes:

In the distance far,
Wanders that bright star,
    Over hill and dale;
To my distant home,
As an envoy roam.
    With my song of wail.

In pris'n and alone.
I my lot bemoan,
  And know not one bright hour,
To stars alone I breathe,
How gladly would I leave,
  Had I but the power.

The stranger listened attentively, and with the greatest excitement, to the song, which was not unknown to him. Tears flowed from his eyes and his hands were pressed to his bosom, as if to suppress his violent feelings.

The prisoner, who had paused some moments, raised his voice again, only to express his feelings in other words. His pale face appeared at a window of the tower and his looks were turned to the stars while he sang the following:

Stars that fade away,
Stay a moment, stay!
  My friends I long to see —
  If they should ask for me
Lead them on this way.

And leaning his head on his hand he continued

Alas! they travel on
Unto their daily bourn.
  With eagerness and glee,
  Their splendour in the sea
They dip and are forlorn.

„My king, oh my king!" sobbed the minstrel. „Oh could I tell him: how near his friends are. — The harp, the harp!" cried he suddenly anp grasping it he with trembling hand but masterly skill played a melody which he once composed for his friend.

Scarce had he finished the first strophe when the prisoner caught up the melody and continued the song. The minstrel's eyes roved over the building for the purpose of discovering the place, whence the well-known sounds came. Perceiving the king he cautiously swung his bonnet, as a sign of recognition.

„Blondel!“ exclaimed the king, but instead of replying, the minstrel seized his harp and sung the following romance:

> „O Richard, O my king,
> „The world abandons thee
> „And no one is seeking,
> „To deliver thee, but me.
>
> „Thy chains I soon will sever
> „And with my song and sword
> „To deliver thee from danger
> „I pledge my life and word!“*)

---

*) We subjoin the text of the French original:

> „O Richard, o mon roi,
> „L'univers t'abandonne,
> „Il n'y a plus que moi,
> „Pour sauver ta personne.
>
> „Je veux rompre tes fers,
> „Et si j'en ai la chance,
> „Mes chansons et mes vers.
> „Fêt'ront ta delivrance.“

Blondel reflected the whole night, how to liberate his king and upon consideration, the best plan seemed to wait for an opportunity to take the castle by surprise. After having reflected upon this plan more closely he resolved, to procure an entrance into the castle at any price and to effect it more easily he thought, the best thing would be, to enter into a more intimate connexion with the maid, whose image had, since their first interview, made a deep inpression upon him.

As unkindly, as he had been received the previous evening, as abruptly and ungraciously was the minstrel's horse ordered to be saddled for his departure the next morning.

Thus pressed, the minstrel could stay no longer and prepared to take his leave. But before he mounted his horse, he found an opportunity of speaking to the maid alone and his words must have touched her heart very deeply; for when he at parting softly whispered to her: „To night!“ she gently pressed his hand and uttered a tender: „Yes!“ whereby a charming expression of embarrassment overspread her features.

Blondel, who did not intend leaving the environs of the castle aligthed at an inn, situated on the road, leading to Annweiler and which seemed to him the most favourable place for watching the castle.

The landlord, an agreeable, portly man, arranged his best room for his guest and after having heard, that the knight had come from the castle, he without being asked related to him all that he knew about it.

„I am well acquainted with the people of Triefels,“ said he with marked self complacency, „the keeper as well as his yeomen come very often to drink their wine here and if you would like to become better acquainted with them you could not have chosen a more favourable opportunity, as our newly elected emperor will be crowned at Frankfort in a few days, upon which occasion the garrison of the castle will celebrate the event in my house.“

„Why! That happens most luckily,“ replied the minstrel, — „and as I once served in the emperor's army, I will partake of the feast given, to his honour and pay for all the wine, drunk on that day. — But that the wine may not be inferior, I will myself select the best you have and lock it up till the festival, as the emperor's health must only be drunk in wines worthy of his name.“

The bargain was made and the best cask of wine selected, to be given to the garrison of the castle on the day of coronation. Blondel then withdrew, for the purpose of forming his plan of deliverance and confiding it to his companions.

The day passed away in this manner and at the approach of night Blondel wrapped himself in his richly folded cloak and ascended the mountain, to take a view of the outworks of the castle and also perform a sweeter duty. After having walked round the castle for some time, he began one of his songs, at the sound of which a bow-window opened and a female head nodded joyfully to him.

It dissappeared immediately after, but only, to appear again through a little side-door, which led from the interior of the castle into the fields.

The loving maid had succeeded in possessing herself of the key, at the view of which the minstrel's heart bounded. He pressed the blushing maid to his breast and returned her his thanks in innumerable kisses.

Hours passed away in their pleàsant tête à tête, till at last the maid was obliged to return, but not without first having promised, to meet her lover again on the following day.

The day of coronation approached. On the evening muffled figures slunk into a wood near the castle and hid themselves in the bushes. They seemed to intend a surprise: for the clinking of arms was sometimes audible from the thick foliage.

In the castle nothing of this proceeding was observed and not a living soul dreamt, that the wood had become a haunt for warriors, who had good reasons to remain undiscovered, — All devoted themselves to the festivities of the day and even the keeper's face appeared less morose.

The draw-bridge at last fell and the warriors hastened merrily to the inn, where the dinner-table was dressed for them and the precious wine stood ready in clean and glittering tin goblets. And when the landlord related to his guests the generosity of the strange knight at the same time extolling the excellent qualities of the wine chosen, their joy knew no bounds and with loud cheers to the emperor and the knight, numerous goblets of the costly beverage were emptied.

Blondel meanwhile walked in expectation up and down before the little side-door, from which his sweet-heart every evening emerged. The most painful and violent impatience stirred his mind and reflected itself in his looks, which he directed from time to time towards the wall, which enclosed the dearest his heart possessed — his friend and his lady-love.

The hour had long passed away, in which he was wont to see her, and he was just reflecting, what to do, if, contrary to all expectation, she should be detained, when suddenly the side-door opened and the maid appeared.

She threw herself on her lovers' breast and communicated to him, that her uncle had stayed

up longer than usual and had before retiring once
more examined, if all accesses were well guarded.

„But he did not think of the side-door,“ said
she jestingly and smiling sweetly, — „which is
indeed quite unnecessary since we guard it.“

The minstrel drew the maid closer and communicated to her with hasty words the reason
which had led him hither. „The time is favourable“, added he, „my warriors are waiting for my
signal, to enter the castle by force and deliver
the king. Return then with me to my native
country and my love shall be your reward.

At the same time and before the surprised
maid could reply, he beckoned towards the wood,
from the shadows of which dark figures appeared
and thronged through the opened side-door.

„Ha, traitor! Then love was not your aim?“
„Oh, forgive me!“
„Woe to me! My uncle, my poor uncle!“

In vain Blondel endeavoured to calm the
alarmed maid; she turned away from him and
fled into the castle. — The minstrel followed
for the cry of war in the castle reminded him
of his duty.

The resistance of the few soldiers, who, in
the absence of their comrades but poorly guarded
the castle, was soon broken. With drawn swords
the besiegers entered the keeper's room, seized
the keys and opened the prisons.

King Richard, hearing the English war cry, stood in joyful excitement in the middle of his room, when suddenly its door flew open and Blondel threw himself into his arms.

„Thanks, many thanks noble lords and friends“, — began the king with the deepest emotion, — „never will I forget your fidelity, and sooner shall my name be forgotten, than my gratitude for your valiant deed. But now give me arms, arms; for they shall not take me alive.“

During this speech the keeper was led into their presence. who even then did not lay off the morose haughtiness which characterized him.

·I protest against this deed, which is contrary to the laws of nations,“ — cried he, a soon as he perceived the armed king, — „and swear to you, that you shall not leave Germany unhurt.“

The maid now hastened forward and accused herself before her uncle of having unconsciously favoured the attack.

Blondel and even the king, who now guessed the reason, endeavoured to calm the frigtened maid; but her thoughts seemed to be in confusion and only directed to her uncle, who heard the confession with a calm, but all the more dangerous rage.

The report of the castle's attack soon spread to the inn and roused the soldiers from their banquet. Hastily they returned, to assist their oppressed companions, but when arrived before the castle they found themselves shut out and menaced.

They assembled to deliberate, in which manner they could best succour their brethren; whereupon the castellan was led upon the rampart and it was announced to them, that, if they dit not retire and remain quiet, his head would be the penalty. They obeyed the call and let the strangers march off undisturbed.

Blondel and even the king did their utmost, to persuade the maid, to accompany them to England. But she firmly refused and renounced the man, who had abused her love. With deep regret he was obliged to leave her, but not without having given her a gold ring and chain, as a token, that he would never forget her.

* * *

Many years had passed, when one fine summer-morning a cavalier rode the same way, which many years ago the English had travelled to seek their king. He reined in his horse at a spot, dangerously overhung by red sand-stone rocks, pushed the gray hairs off his forehead and exlaimed: „Here is the place, where the shepherd once sung; and to this place is attached the remembrance of the greatest bliss and the deepest woe, which I ever felt in all my life!“

Saying this he sank into a deep meditation, from which he was roused by a voice singing the same air, as sung by king Richard in Triefels.

The old man started: a tear stole from his eye and ran down into his beard.

Slowly he rode onward and took the way to Triefels. When he arrived at the inn, where the soldiery of the castle had once celebrated the coronation of the emperor, he alighted and ordered a room.

By a singular coincidence the same room was appointed to him, which he had formerly occupied and after having contemplated it with deep emotion, he looked into the face of the landlord and recognized the shepherd's boy, whom he had enabled with his gold, to buy the inn from its former possessor.

With tender interest the old man — in whom the reader may recognize Blondel — enquired about the castellan and his niece. He was told, that the former had, soon after the king's flight, been killed by some hidden hand and the latter had entered the nunnery of Eberstein about four miles and a half from Baden.

Heidelberg.

Whoever has visited the beautifully situated town of Heidelberg presumably also the castle and its environs, must have observed the name of a prophetess of ancient Germany connected with various places.

The „Jettebühl", the „Wolfsbrunnen" and the place, on which the Jetta-temple once stood, now occupied by the „Friedrichsbau", are all monuments, which remind one of her and the tragical death she suffered.

The following tradition gives us an account of her.

A beautiful prophetess had established herself in a grove, which was consecrated to Hertha, and who made the people around her happy with her counsels and advice

She was incomparably lovely and in her soft and deep-blue eyes there seemed to reign peace and wisdom; all who came within her presence became mute with astonishment and reverence.

The report of her wisdom and the infallibility
of her prophecies spread over all the neighbouring and even distant countries and allured many
youths and men, to learn from her lips the secret
of their destiny.

Many there were indeed who would have liked
to have lead her as a consort into their paternal
halls; but such a wish was never uttered in her
presence, for the maid was serious in her manners and her solitary life lent her an air which
commanded awe and respect from all who approached her.

Lost in meditation she once sat upon the
steps of the altar, on which she had kindled a
little fire, which cast a faint light around causing her and the trees around to look like spectres,
when just then steps rustling through the foliage
betrayed a new-comer, and a tall young man
stepped forth from the shadows of the evening
before the maid.

„You have,“ began he, „the gift of reading
the destinies of man in your magic figures and
I too am come, to hear my fate from your lips.“

The maid, aroused from her musings, looked
up at him and when her eyes met his, a light
unnoticed by him, flashed in them, which betrayed
confusion and spread in blushes over her face.

The youth was transfix'd with astonishment;
for female beauty and female looks had never

before made such an impression upon him, as in this case and in embarrassment he stood opposite the prophetess, not knowing, what to say. Thus they remained for some time, looking at one another in silence and as it were, reading each others thoughts.

„Youth", said the maid, having regained her self-command, „you have come at an hour, when the spirit of prophecy has deserted me and I should be obliged, to make a sacrifice to Hertha, to enable me to reveal the mystery of my signs, come again to morrow; I shall then give you an answer; to day I can not!"

„I will certainly return to morrow and with pleasure; for I leave more here behind than the future promises.

Without waiting for the maid's reply, he hastened away! and from the darkness of the wood, and the shadows of the oaks, he looked back once more upon the lovely sight.

The next day he returned and found the prophetess in the same attitude, as the day before.

He approached her respectfully bent his knee and kissed the hem of her dress.

The maid allowed this and a look of satisfaction lit up her face, as she perceived the reverence of the youth, whose image had so wonderfully filled her heart with love. As if in the act of blessing him she laid her hand upon his head and said in a low and trembling voice, which betrayed her excitement:

"You have come, to hear your fortune?"

"Not from the prophetess", replied the youth, "but from the lips of one I love!" added he softly.

The maid was not angry, even when he drew her hand to his lips and looking up, he perceived her absorbed in deep thought and tears in her eyes.

"Hertha will punish me for not having guarded my heart better. — She must forgive me! I am in love!"

"You love me?" exclaimed the youth joyfully. "Oh, heavenly maid, how can I reward you for the bliss, which I derive from those words? — Oh weep not; Hertha may vent her anger on me; for I am strong and the Gods know my courage in battle, but you, added he, entwining her tenderly in his arms you shall be my "Walkyre" and lead me to the regions where heroes banquet and bards sing their praises and there pour me out Wodans mead. — Oh, come with me; you will bring me bliss and I will make you as happy, as a tender-loving heart can. Freya will sweeten our life and appease Hertha by her offerings."

"No, No!" replied the prophetess softly shaking her head. Our love must be concealed by the shadows of night, for a priestess of Hertha dare not be man's wife and an inmate of his house. If you love me, return often, very often, and lest nobody should surprise us, I will wait for you at the rivulet, where it branches off in five directions running into five different ponds, in which I consecrate offerings to Hertha: there we are safe from observation and can enjoy our love undisturbed!"

Thankful and happy the young man swore to return and at the solicitation of the prophetess he departed promising to see her again on the following day.

The next evening arrived and full of happiness, and expectation he hastened with winged steps to the place of meeting. Arrived at the appointed spot he there saw his beloved stretched on the ground and a huge wolf, with fangs full of gore, tearing out her heart.

With a yell of rage he rushed upon the monster and thrust his sword into its jaws, killing it immediately. He then stooped down, raised the life-less head of his mistress and called her tenderly by name. In vain! Hertha had punished her faithless priestess!

In Heidelbergs grand hall,
When in its glorious days;
There was a jester small,
Renown'd for his quaint ways.

His thirst was great and that
Beyond discription so —
Once to the monster vat
The pages made him go.

Unto that Monarch grand
Who proudly there does reign,
Whose spirit mighty bland,
Is perfume of old wine.

Ha! ha; bethought the fool,
How stupid would it be
To leave this cellar cool —
For ever part from thee. —

No! no! — I am sincere,
I care not to return;
My heaven is center'd here,
My throat with thirst does burn.

Then quick a gimlet drew,
And bored until it ran
And drank — and drank anew
'Till all before him swam.

Then down he sank and slept;
And dreamt of Paradise.
As o'er him gaily lept
That stream he thought so nice.

The pages who had brought him
Listen'd quietly and long,
Until fear o'ercame them,
With thoughts of something wrong.

Then carefully and slow,
All hand in hand they crept,
Unto the fool below,
Who peacefully still slept.

He slept the sleep of peace —·
— Had drown'd himself in wine.
The smile that lit his face
Was happiness divine.

———————

Auerbach.

As most people are prone to believe that old castles and ancient strongholds contain hidden treasures, so may we imagine them to contain hidden and decayed wine-cellars, since in ancient times wine was regarded as a gift of the Gods and consequently carefully treasured.

The Greeks and Romans consecrated a particular God to it, the poets sang its praises and others drank it. Wine-cellars are very desirable places and it is not to be wondered at, if people took the trouble to build them and enjoy their contents.

A peasant once passing the castle of Auerbach must have been inspired with the same idea, as he viewed the vineyards on the surrounding hills and exclaimed mournfully; „If one only had that which in former times was wantonly destroyed and wasted!" Whereupon a short stout old man, with a leather-apron round his waist, suddenly stood before him and looked at him with eyes beaming with good humour.

„'Would'st like to refresh thyself in the wine of the great, I guess?! — Come along with me and I will gratify you; we can then pass a pleasant hour together.“

„Lead the way, sir; I will follow; for I can not refuse such a kind offer!“

At that moment a sweet fragrance of wine assailed his nose and intoxicated his senses beforehand.

The cooper tripped through vines, hedges of thorns and over broken walls, till he arrived at a decayed cellar-door, where he invited the peasant to descend the rotten, and partly with gray moss covered, steps.

When they had arrived at the bottom, he took a candle, a syphon and a mighty bowl from a niche in the wall and led the guest over the moist and slippery ground into the depht of the long and hollow resounding vaults.

They had not proceeded far, when, by the feeble glimmer of the candle-light, a gigantic tun appeared from out the darkness and the cooper began with loving tenderness to relate, that they were now in his kingdom, where the subjects peaceably waited for their deliverance through him.

At the same time he held the candle so, that

his guest could peer in to the dephts of the cellar,
wherein a long row of tuns lay, one beside
another, in calm contentment, till the last disappeared in darkness.

„You all-bountiful!“ exclaimed the peasant
astonished and rejoiced, at the same time, clapping
his hands. „Why, such a grand collection of
the best gifts of nature I never saw before, and
the tuns glitter like pure gold.“

„Truly so!“ smiled the cooper, the reason is,
because the wine has formed its own cask; for
those, which man made, are rotten and decayed
long ago. But come along, to look at them is
not sufficient, we must taste them and then you
must tell me, if you ever found a wine like mine.

There upon he applied the syphon, filled the
bowl and drank to the peasant.

The peasant drank the fragrant fluid with
mighty draughts and having emptied the bowl,
he smacked his lips with an air of satisfaction.

„That is a magnificent wine“, cried he with
rapture; indeed I never drank better: oh, how
delicious.

„Go forward, you will find it better still;
that was only an inferior one, farther back is
my better sort.“

Thus they wandered from cask to cask and
it was not long, before the peasant began to
cry and howl, embrace the casks, kiss them and

appear quite enamoured with their contents. But the cooper laughed and said at every new goblet.

„Oh, that is nothing! There is something better coming!“

And better still came; for when the peasant had tried the last cask and had even emptied a glass there of filled to the brim, his tears gushed more abundantly; he became giddy and sinking down he fell into a deep slumber.

When he awoke the next morning, he found himself in a ditch behind the ruin and as soon as he had recovered his senses sufficiently, he sought for the entrance to the cellar but in vain! he could not find it.

Since then many have sought for it, but no one could ever discover it. Some can at times inhale such a fragrant perfume of wine, when passing that way that they exclaim one to another:

„The cooper is tasting his wine!“

Frankfort o. M.

t the end of the Eschenheimer-street in Frankfort o. M. stands a tower surmounted by five tall points, the centre one of which is furnished with a vane, in which nine round holes form the number 9.

The tradition of the origin of these holes tells us, that once a notorious poacher sat as a prisoner in the tower, awaiting his judgment. He was a famous shot and though they could not impute any grave crime to him, yet his poaching was sufficient to bring down upon him a high penalty.

Gloomy and dejected the prisoner sat in his cell, with his back turned to the rays of the sun, which penetrated through the crated window into his room and seemed to call him out upon the verdant plains, where every one, busily and cheerily, enjoyed its warm rays; the sun and the poacher were old acquaintances and as the latter would not turn his face to the sun, his rays grew visibly paler and withdrew slowly and sadly up until it disappeared through the window.

Discontented with himself and the whole world the prisoner sunk upon the boards and tried to sleep.

He at last succeeded and pleasant must have been his dreams, for a cheerful expression spread over his features; but on a sudden they were contracted by rage, he struggled with hands and feet and grinding his teeth mutter'd. „Ha, you villain, that was a trap!“ His distorted features changed into painful sadness; they once more contracted, as he muttered something indistinctly, at the same time moving restlessly on his couch and compressing his fingers, like one whose mind was troubled. But this expression vanished; bold resolution pictured itself on his face and his breast heaved as with a proud consciousness of his strenght.

Just then the prison-door opened and the turnkey with a rough shake roused him from his dreams, so that he, at first dit now know, where he was.

He however soon became aware of his position; for two messengers from the high council stood before him and read his sentence of death, which comdemned him to be hanged.

After having heard the sentence he began:

„That is a sin, gentlemen, for I did nothing but kill those animals, which were given to us all for our use. An animal is but an animal and on its account to kill a man, is a crime, which must be answered before God."

„You are known as a dangerous poacher," replied one of the judges, „and your comrades as well as the praiseworthy company of foresters accuse you of being in league with the devil and from him procuring charmed bullets."

„It 's false, and to prove it, I offer to shoot in public and with blessed powder and bullets nine shots through the vane of the tower, which shall form a number."

„Ah, if you can perform that, you will remove the chief motive of your sentence. But reflect well for you challenge the Most-High, whom none dare deride with impunity!"

„I can do it!" replied the hunter proudly. „for I am innocent and excepting a few wild pranks my conscience charges me with no crime!"

The report of this proposal spread like lightning through the town and the inhabitants, as well as the foresters who interested themselves in his fate, and whose sympathy he had won by the marvellous confidence he exhibited in his own skill, forced themselves into the council and insisted upon the pardon of the hunter, if he carried out his assertion.

The hunter was informed, that judges would witness his skill and if he suceeded in verifying his assertion, he would be pardoned and set at liberty. But if one bullet missed or failled in forming the number, he must certainly die.

The hunter agreed and the next day was the day fixed for his trial of skill.

The following morning an immense crowd thronged around the foot of the tower, which at that time was still joined with the town-rampart and accessible therefrom; the guild of foresters ranged themselves upon the wall and their master prepared to cast the bullets, which should decide the prisoner's fate.

He was led forth at last and again addressed by a monk, who admonished him, not to tempt God, if his skill was only founded on the assist-ance of the devil.

„Have patience, reverend father", replied the hunter, „with the help of God and St. Hubert I will write my answer to that on the weather-cock of the tower."

The master of foresters loaded the gun and handed it to him.

Deep silence hovered over the assembly, as the prisoner took his gun and prepared to fire; but when after the report, the creaking and shinning of the vane indicated, that he had shot a hole through it the multitude gave vent to their feelings in loud shouts of joy and caps and hats ware waved.

The hunter prepared to fire again. All were breathless. After the report the vane turned again and a second hole was visible, which also was hailed with loud and long hurras.

Nine times the hunter fired and nine times the bullets hit the mark, which he assigned them. After having fired the last bullet, and completed the figure 9 he sank on his knees and all, who were present, bared their heads and joined him in prayer from the depht of their hearts.

On the evening of the same day the hunter, loaded with presents, walked through the archway of that tower which had been the scene of his skill, and from that time on he became a highly respected forester. He never returned to Frankfort after; its memory had become detestabe to him.

The colony of the Jews.

A mong the Roman soldiers, who destroyed Jerusalem, there served a lord of Dalberg, whose hereditary castle at Hernsheim near Worms is still inhabited by his descendants. It has been through time changed, enlarged and improved. It is useles to enter into particulars, as the legend we have to mention has little to do with the castle and its fate.

The above-mentioned Dalberg was centurion and received as booty a number of Jewis prisoners, which he took with him into his native country, to found a colony.

These were the first Jews in Germany. Painful was the departure of the unhappy prisoners, bereft of their home and goods by the war. But in order, not to loose all remembrance of their home, they filled sacks with earth and took them as holy relics into the distant country, that after their death at last they could be buried in native ground.

Among the captives was distinguished an old man, who, guided by his lovely daughter, blooming with all the charms of innocence, tottered mournfully into the foreign country.

He was a wise man, filled with a strong confidence in God, and he, like his daughter, instilled by advice and deed new hope and courage in to their desolate fellow prisoners, reminding them of Jehovah's omnipotence.

A more beautiful contrast could not be imagined, than the old man led by the lovely girl; it seemed, as if nature autumn wandered hand in hand with blooming spring, and the serene tranquillity which both displayed, excited such a veneration, that even the soldiers during the long journey became more affable and abstained from coarse jests.

Soon after the arrival of the Jews at Worms the lord of Dalberg arrived also, to recover in his castle from the hardships of the Jewish war. His neighbours and friends came from far and near to hear the recital of his adventures and those of the Roman army from the lips of an eye-witness, and huntingparties, banquets and entertainments of all kinds followed each other in quick succession.

Among the guests, who most frequently visited the castle of the centurion, was a distinguished Roman officer, who belonged to a cohort of the garrison of Mayence, stationed there for guarding the borders of the empire against the Germans. He was rich and noble and had been for a long time one of Dalberg's most intimate friends.

He was a worldly man and had no sooner seen the lovely but unfortunate Jewess than he began to consider the best plan to obtain possesion of her.

To buy her from Dalberg was impossible, as he would not agree with it.

Only one chance remained that was to run away with her; no sooner thought of, than determined upon. For this purpose he prepared a place of refuge, hidden in a deep forest, in the vicinity of Mayence and then rode towards Worms, where he saw the maid, as she was fetching water, seized her, and in spite of her resistance leapt with her upon the horse and galloped off.

The Roman tried everything in his power to induce her to look favourably upon him but without avail. Neither kind words nor rich presents could prevail upon her to deviate from the part of virtue.

Irritated at last by the maid's obstinacy, as he called it, and aware that searches, were being made for the stolen one, resolved one evening to compel her to submit to his proposals.

Just returned from a bacchanalian orgie, which he had celebrated with some friends, he hastened to his prisoner and again tried his persuasions but in vain!

"You shall not escape me, little prude!" said he. Excited with wine and passion, he seized her and tried to kiss her; but the maid struggled from him and as he became more excited and continued his importunities she fell on her knees and invoked God to protect her.

"A curse on your God!" cried the Roman. "Mine you must be, and if it cost my life!" So saying he rushed upon the helpless girl and was about to violate her when with a loud peal of thunder a flaming stone fell and killed him.

The maid was saved, but when she looked at the instrument of her deliverance, the features of Jehovah shone therefrom with such a dazzling brilliancy that she became blind.

Dalberg and her father discovered the maid at last, who through her misfortune had become more lovely, and when she told them, what had happened they wondered and looked with reverence and awe at the stone, on which the name of Jehovah was engraved in Hebrew letters, but which was now without the splendour that blinded the maid.

The unhappy maid and her old father died a few months after this event, within a short time of eachother. They were the first Jews who were buried in Germany.

6*

It is said that the stone at a later period, adorned the ceiling of the Synagogue in Worms.

It is worth mentioning, that the earth which they took with them from Judea is still to be found, they say, in a particular spot of the Jewish burial-ground at Worms.

The daughter
of the castellan of Worms.

A s one leaves the railway-Station and
passes through the gate, turning to the
left, arrives at a large square, enclosed
by chains, opposite to which stands
on old manorhouse, built in the renaissance-style
and called „Wampolder Hof.“

This structure, which at present is divided
into two properties, once belonged to one of the
most distinguished patricians of Mayence, the
lord of Wampold, and was inhabited by a castellan, who was charged with its preservation.

The castellan himself was a nobleman, whose
estates had been mortgaged long ago and who
had, as a kinsman of the family of Wampold,
obtained this post through favour. He was old
and infirm, having in his young days been in
many campaigns and now only found consolation
for the vanities of the past in his young daughter,

who, in the freshness of youth, was one of the most beaufitul among her companions.

No wonder therefore, that many young gentlemen wooed the beauty and hovered about her, like butterflies around flowers. But no wonder also, that these attentions made her somewhat capricious, for a maid, flattered by many lovers, can seldom retain those most charming qualities, naturalness and simplicity.

Among the youths who endeavoured to please her only one gained her especial favour and he was of good family like herself but poor and the only son of an old widow.

He was slender and nobly formed and outshone by piety, courage and a cultivated mind all those superficial fellows, who relying upon the power of their riches, neglect to acquire the true treasures, virtue and education.

The maid, although spoiled and capricious, loved him sincerely and their happiness seemed founded, as the father approved of their love and betrothed her to the youth.

One night — it happened to be the Walpurgis night — in the little society of young people in the „Wampolder Hof“ many stories of witches and witchcraft had been told. When the keepers daughter suddenly formed the idea of imposing upon her lover the task of watching, at midnight where the roads cross; the procession of

witches and give her a description of it afterwards. The youth laughingly promised, for he
was courageous and believed that a Christian,
conscious of no guilt, could never be harmed by
witchcraft. Defenceless he rapidly strode to the
neighbouring field and never returned.

At the report of this horrible event the mother
of the missed youth cursed the silly maid, who
went mad and died, but every Walpurgis night
as is said she runs about the town, calling
anxiously for he lover.

How and where the youth disappeared, could
never be ascertained. Some believed, the witches
had torn him to pieces and scattered his limbs
in the air, but others, more sensible, thought,
his rivals had murdered him and thrown him into
the Rhine, which last opinion seems most pro-
bable; as the fishermen of the Rhine some time
after found a corpse, whose swollen limbs appeared
to be those of the unhappy youth.

Worms.

Amongst other things of interest attached to the vicinity I must mention the Rosengarten (garden of roses); a meadow situated opposite Worms on the right bank of the Rhine and made popular by being mentioned in the famed song of the „Nibelungen“.

Another spot mentioned in the above song is the Drachenfels near Dürkheim on the Haardt on which rock Siegfried killed the dragon which desolated the surrounding country.

Then again Worms is celebrated for its wine called „Liebfrauenmilch“ which grows around the church of „Our blessed Lady“ of Liebe Frau and is supposed to derive its name from the following legend:

An old nobleman of Burgundy was very fond of wine, but on the other hand was pious and gave generously to the poor.

This vexed the arch fiend, who in those times was obliged to win souls through cunning and he resolved, to ensnare his soul playing upon his weakness. He disguised himself as a strolling knight, became acquainted with the nobleman and when the other praised the excellent qualities of his wine and placed before Satan a bumper of the excellent juice the latter gave the nobleman such an enticing description of a wine, which according to his statement, he had drunk, in the south, that the inveterate wine-drinker promised any thing, if his guest could procure him a wine like the one he had described.

The stranger promised to plant a similar vineyard for the knight, on the condition of the forfeiture of his soul. The vineyard grew as if by magic and the produce of the first vintage was so luscious, that the nobleman, in a moment of ecstacy occasioned by liberal potations christened it, in spite of the devil's admonitions „Liebfrauenmilch" (Milk of our blessed Lady), meaning thereby that better could not be found.

At hearing that name, the devil looked furious indeed; but he consoled himself with the hope of possessing the knight's soul. But in this he was also mistaken, for the „good Lady", who felt pity for the good-hearted and pious knight and wished to return her thanks for the dedication of the vine-yard, just at the time when the devil was about to realize his bond, sent some angels, who drove him away. But the knight, who had learned by this circumstance, how wine may endanger ones salvation, built a small chapel in his vineyard to the honour of the „Blessed Lady“ and for many years is supposed to have enjoyed, under her protection, the devil's delicious wine.

Every one will agree, that the „Liebfrauenmilch“ deserves the latter appellation; but I leave the reader to decide, whether it was really planted by the devil or not as the tradition says it was.

———————

Oppenheim.

 ne evening a young painter arrived in Oppenheim, which is situated near the banks of the Rhine and entered an inn, at the door of which at that moment appeared the curly head of a beautiful young girl, who looked smilingly at the strolling artist.

„That happens luckily", thought the painter, „for if in entering a town the first object one meets is a girl, it forbodes good, I will not be deaf to this call of fortune and shall remain here.

Thus saying he entered and the maid blushingly withdrew.

„Good evening, fair maid!" exclaimed the painter afterwards in the tap-room „Grant me a lodging in your house and a kind look from your sweet eyes. I come a great distance, am weary and long for refreshment of the body as well as rest."

Smilingly the maid listened to the cheerful speech of the new-comer, and when he had finished, she bowed and asked, what his wishes were.

„A bed room and as we cannot subsist on the perfume of roses and sunshine, I would like something more substantial, for example a chicken and a glass of wine!"

„You shall have both!" replied the maid smiling and hastening away, to give the necessary orders.

The painter looked after her and as soon as she had disappeared, he said: „Hm, she does not seem to take much notice of my words. But beautiful she is indeed, and I will have her in my portfolio; if she accepts her payment in kisses, she shall have my whole store of them."

Singing and whistling he walked up and down the room, till a boy brought him the key of his chamber, with the remark, that he had been charged to show him to it.

„Here boy, take this money and buy your sweet-heart something; a ribbon or a such like bauble, for I guess you have a sweet-heart too it being the fashion now."

The boy put the piece of money in his pocket with a smile and such a sly look, that the painter laughed loudly.

Arrived in his small, but pretty room, he made himself comfortable, eat and drank what was served him, took from his travelling bag a change, brushed himself and arranged his long, flowing hair before the looking glass.

After having again examined his toilette and found it in order, he hastened down into the garden, where he met the landlord's charming daughter, watering the flowers.

"Are you come to help me?" asked she at seeing him.

"Certaily, queen of roses or better said Undine!"

"Whose fountain is the watering-pot", interrupted the maid jesting.

, "Be it so, if it only flows!" replied the youth, seizing the vessel and amid jokes and merriment soon became absorbed in his work.

The maid, was not all afraid of this merry fellow, but returned his jests in like manner and they soon began laughing and running about the garden, throwing rose-leaves and water at each other. After having concluded peace, they walked quietly through the garden together and conversed about the beauties and curiosities of the "environs", when the maid was informed, that her admirer was a painter, about to visit and sketch the finest points of the Rhine.

"Oh, then be so kind, as to sketch my dear Oppenheim also!" entreated the maid, half jesting, half serious. "The ruins must be very beautiful; by moonlight and also the houses in the town below, peaceably reposing in slumber."

"Why not in sunlight? I would then have the

opportunity of embellishing the picture with your lovely portrait!" said the painter laughing.

"No, no: the picture must be romantic and will not be so, if it contains my portrait!"

"Well I shall visit the ruins at night and I promise to copy them faithfully."

"And shall I also have a copy?"

"You shall have the original; in that you will be happier, than I."

"Who knows?" replied she, blushing and with a nod sprang away.

The youth walked at night fall towards the ruins of the church, which still contains the bones of the soldiers, who fell in the thirty-years war at Oppenheim. The moon illumined the decayed walls with a ghastly light and the wind blew through the foliage of the trees. A gloomy silence reigned over the bedewed fields; and the steps of the traveller sounded hollowly through the night.

Absorbed in melancholy thoughts at the view of the ruins, which appeared in the light of the moon most terribly weird, he walked on, till his foot knocked against a skull, which rolled with a hollow sound over the ground and stooped with its grinning face upwards.

"Decay and putrefaction", exclaimed the youth sighing, "are all, that remains of wordly pomp and splendour! All vanishes except the glory", added he with ardour, „and happy he, who gains it!"

Meditating thus he had wandered through the building for some time, when the moon suddenly became overclouded; at that moment it struck midnight; and hearing a noise behind him, he turned round and with horror saw, that the bones joined and formed skeletons.

Scarce were the skeletons upright on their shaky legs, than they separated; the Swedes joined the Swedes and the Spaniards the Spaniards. The word of command was uttered in a hoarse voice, upon which they attacked each other furiously.

At this horrible sight, the young man, covered with a cold perspiration, supported himself against the wall. His teeth chattered and his limbs seemed no longer able to support his body.

However the fighting of this army of skeletons became more and more furios. Many of both parties sank sighing and moved no more. One of these skeletons, the skull of which had received the kick, fell at the feet of the young man, uttering woeful cries. When its dark and hollow eyes by chance met those of the young man, a light seemed to come from them and it exclaimed sighing and threatening:

„Mortal, who viewed the combat of the dead, tell to all how we are forced to persecute each other even after death, because instead of loving each another during life, we were enemies. Alas, we shall find no rest, until we are buried!"

These words were scarcely uttered, when the clock struck one and the skeletons ceased fighting.

When the young man, recovered from his deadly fear, he hurried away and did not recover his tranquility, until he arrived at the inn, where the maiden received and consoled him for what he had endured. On the next day the bones where found in wild disorder, dispersed here and there and when shortly after the seven-years' war broke out the people of Oppenheim said, it had been foretold by the apparition of the skeletons.

The painter often resorted to the ruins and related the circumstance to his wife, and she as often described how pale and terrified he looked on his return. The reader will easily recognize in her the pretty maid, whose view had seemed to the painter an omen of good luck; for, though he had not gained eternal glory, at least he in his household enjoyd constant happiness, founded upon love and confidence.

The maiden-leap.

In former times, when giants were still in existence and men not only had to combat against their own passions, but also against the evils of those monsters, one of them lived in the Haardtmountains.

He built a fortress upon the top of a high mountain, from the tower of which he could survey the whole country. It so happened that some miles distant from him lived a beautiful damsel, who was as courageous as she was graceful and spiritual. She inhabited an abandoned castle: she rode, hunted and took great delight in such-like manly exercises. However at home she managed her household very cleverly and showed as much skill at her spinning-wheel, as in bending the bow, whose arrows rarely missed their aim.

One day the young girl happened to meet the giant; he instantly formed the resolution, of possessing her. He reflected for a long time upon the manner to be pursued, and the more

7

he thought of her, the more her image charmed
him and unsettled his mind; he wanderd through
his castle in the greatest excitement and sleep
forsook him.

At lenght not able to endure it any longer,
he called his trusty servant, gave him a quantity
of valuable jewels as presents for the maid and
charged him, to urge his suit with her.

The servant, a cunning fellow, thought to
himself, on his way to the maid's castle: „Why
should I give all these precious things to the maid
and perhaps bring back a refusal? That would
be folly indeed and it is much better for me
to keep the jewels as a reward for my journey
and bring him a refusal at once."

After having thus reflected, he left the road
and entered a forest for the purpose of seeking
a hiding-place for the treasures, which he had
received for the maid.

Having advanced far into the forest, he
suddenly saw a youth wringing his hands and
weeping.

„Ah!" said the servant to himself: „This
young man may give me more accurate information about the country and even show the
way to the maid's castle, that I may hear from
her own lips, her message to the giant." And
having said so, he called the young man who
looked at the stranger with astonishment, at

the same time putting his hand to his sword, for greater security.

„Don't be afraid!“ cried the dishonest messenger, „I am a stranger and am looking for a quiet, lonely place, where I could rest myself.“

„If that is, what you wish, I can show you a secret place, for I am always ready to offer strangers my poor services.“

He left go of his sword and offered his hand to the stranger, who grasped it rejoiced, to have found a guide.

On the way the young man related his misfortune and narrated, that he was in love with a young girl, whom he dared not approach on account of his poverty.

The cunning fellow soon perceived from the young mans words; that the fire, which consumed his heart, had been kindled by the same eyes, which had inflamed the heard of his lord. A malicious smile played over his face, for he was thinking of a horrible plan, how to keep the treasures and still receive from his master a large reward for his fidelity.

After having reflected upon it, he confided to the young man, that he was in possession of a treasure, which he intended to bury. „Help me“, said he, „and you shall have a share of it, which will enable you, to marry your beloved maid.“ The youth agreed with pleasure and when they arrived at the place, they began to work and dug a great hole. The place was solitary and pleasant; there was a large stone, irrigated by a rivulet They both worked hard, but scarce was the hole dug, when the criminal rushed suddenly upon the youth, exclaiming: You must now die, for nobody shall know, where the treasure is hid."

The youth, who suspected no evil, had put his sword upon a stone, for the purpose of not being hindered by it in his work.

The assassain had remarked it and assailed the youth, putting himself between him and the sword. Having previously seen the young man in tears, the robber thought him a coward, but he found his mistake, for scarce had the youth recovered from his surprise, when he suddenly rushed upon the assassin and flung him with such violence on the stone, that he sunk down moaning and nearly fainting. The youth hastened to seize his sword and in his wrath was already about to stab the miserable assassain, when he craved pardon saying, that he had a secret to tell, which would be more agreeable to him, than all the treasures of the world.

The youth felt pity for the cowardly wretch, withdrew his sword and anxious to hear, what he had to communicate, summoned him to speak.

The impostor told him the aim of his journey

and the love of the giant, his lord, for the fair and courageous lady of the castle; observing, that the giant, would go to extremes for the sake of obtaining his object.

„I care not; let him come,“ cried the youth conscious of his strength and passionate love, „I will stand against him, if he dares to attempt anything against her!“

He then took his legitimate share of the treasure, and likewise the horse of the vanquished and withdrew, abandoning the wretch to his fate.

The giant grew impatient: he waited in vain for the return of his messenger and as his passion grew stronger, he resolved to fetch an answer himself. No sooner said, than done. He rose and walked to the castle of his lady-love.

She happened to be sitting among her maids helping them to fold the linen and lay it in order in the cup-board, when it was announced to her, that a giant waited before the gate of the castle and wished to speak to her. Surprised and with a secret feeling of danger she went out on the turret of the castle, as the gate was too narrow for the giant.

„Young lady“, cried the monster, I will marry you and if you don't agree to be my wife, I shall demolish your castle and kill you and all your people.“

The young girl shuddered and melted into

tears, when she reflected upon her horrible destiny. In vain she conjured the giant, to spare her and promised him all her treasures. In vain her maids knelt before him; he laughed at her pain and said, that the tears made her still more beautiful and his passion more violent.

As the giant was inexorable, the maid stepped forth resolutely and saith: „You shall marry me, but all who woo me, must first prove, that they are worthy of me."

„Oh," replied the giant laughing: „you doubt of my strenght? Shall I root up the trees, which overshadow you?" and saying this he grasped a huge lime-tree and pulled it out, as if it were a reed.

The maid replied trembling: „It is not bodily strenght, which inspires me with confidence, but resoluteness and presence of mind in danger."

„Well, let us see, fair maid! What is your desire?"

„Run after me and if you overtake me, I will follow you into your castle."

The wretch smilingly consented to the proposal for he delighted in seeing the maid between hope and fear, before he took her to his castle.

The resolute maid took courage, ordered forth her favourite steed, adorned with the prettiest saddle; she herself put on her finest attire and took leave of her maids as well as of her castle and estates.

„Sooner will I die, than follow this monster; and if God abandons me, and I cannot escape him, I will kill myself, even on the steps of the altar, whither he will drag me!"

Having uttered these words, she once more took leave of her maids, vaulted nimbly upon the horse and galloped away.

The contest in running began; the steed neighed loudly and merrily; as if it were conscious, that the fate of its mistress depended on its swiftness, it ran its best. The giant followed close behind, for the sight of the charming lady and her splendid attire had heated his brain.

They had run many miles and the giant gained upon her gradually; her steed was tired and she gave up the hope of rescue.

Shuddering at the thought of being obliged to wed the monster, she preferred death and spurred her steed to the border of a chasm.

The noble animal made its last effort, leapt over the chasm and arrived luckily at the other side. The giant roaring with rage approached the rock and beheld at the other side the maid kneeling down praying, while her horse grazed calmly by her side, as if nothing had happened. He strode up and down, the border of the chasm, when suddenly a shout of joy announced to the frightened maid, that he had found a passage. He prepared already to profit by it, when a knight, out of breath, arrived bidding the giant stop. Astonished at the boldness of the stranger, the giant remained motionless. The young knight descended from his horse, drew his sword and rushed on the giant, who, already exhausted by the long race, had lost most of his strength. After a terrible combat the giant, near the steep side of the rock, was about to seize a huge stone, with which he meant to kill his adversary, when his foot slipped and he plunged head-foremost into the chasm.

Between fear and hope, the maid had watched the doubtful combat and when as by a miracle it was at last decided and the knight came to meet the anxious maiden, she hastened to him and sank on his breast in tears.

The knight, after having abandoned the wretched messenger in the forest to his unhappy fate, had repaired to the maid, to inform her of the giant's machinations and by that, to gain her favour. On the way he with surprise and indignation saw the race and foreseeing mischief followed them at full gallop and arrived just in time to save her.

The young man again expressing his rapture at her deliverance, begged her to accept him as protector and companion for life; she looked up

at him, her face resplendent with love and gratitude, offered him her hand and withdrew it
not when he pressed it to his lips.

Some days after their jojful return to the
castle, the wedding was celebrated; they lived
long and happily and were blessed with children,
who resembled them in mind and body.

The rock, which was then a barrier to evil,
is to the present time called the „**Maiden's
leap.**"

The vintager's daughter.

pon a rock there stands aloft,
　　A little cottage clean,
From whose window eyes most soft,
　　Peer out with look serene.

A female with fair curly head,
　　Sits pensively and mild;
From her hair the sunbeams shed
　　A halo round the child.

How oft I've stood and linger'd,
　　To watch that creature fair;
As with looks cast heavenward
　　She rivalled any there.

Her image in my boyhood's heart
　　Is firm as firm can be;
Day and night that image bright,
　　Methinks I always see —.

Mayence.

Shortly after the Christian faith had taken firm root in Germany and Roman and Grecian literature had transplanted itself there, monasteries were found to be the only safe asylums for devotees to science and arts.

From these quiet institutions flowed knowledge and as a forerunner of Poetry came the troubadour. In later times, as the minds of the people became more cultivated and delighted more in the simple songs of the minstrel, the poetry of the Mastersinger commenced and the poetical efforts became more general.

The prosperity of the cities added not a little to the popularity of minstrelsy. People established societies for the promulgation of the art and authors of the best songs and verses were rewarded with prizes. Among the founders of those academies and the most renowned in the towns along the Rhine was Henry of Meissen, who flourished in the beginning of the fourteenth century.

His songs, of which a considerable number are still preserved, exhale a noble enthusiasm for female beauty and loveliness. On account of this prevailing character of his songs he was called: „Frauenlob", by which name he is still denominated.

The women and girls of Mayence of that period, who had honoured the panegyrist of their sex during his life, at his decease (1317) showed their veneneration in an extraordinary and touching manner. They prepared obsequies for him, as no other either before, or after had ever received.

At break of the funeral-day the bells of the cathedral rang accompanied by the bells of the other churches. Women and girls of every rank assembled in mourning-dresses and eight ladies of the greatest beauty took the coffin, which was covered with a pall and adorned with myrtles and lilies, upon their shoulders and carried it in funeral pace to the cathedral. A long train of women followed them, mingling their songs with the solemn sound of the bells.

The cathedral was spendidly decorated. The organ sounded mournfully and solemnly through its high vaults. As the funeral procession entered, the sobs and lamentations of the assembly were heard throughout. Deep silence reigned, when the coffin was interred. The archbishop himself gave the benediction and the young ladies strewed the tomb with roses and poured precious wine out of golden goblets into it.

At the closing of the tomb a sacred hymn, which the deceased had composed and dedicated to the fair sex was sung; then a high mass was celebrated, at the conclusion of which the melodius voices of the maids intoned a song, expressing the hope of immortality.

The multitude once more thronged to the tomb and laid their last offerings on it; they then dispersed, in sadness.

The monument, erected to him, was destroyed during the repairs, which were made near it in the year 1744, but by the praiseworthy zeal of professor Niclas Vogt, author of the „history and legends of the Rhine", a new monument, similar to the first, was erected near the same place.

Arnold of Walpoden.

There was a great stir in the ancient town of Mayence. With day-break crowds of men and women in splendid attire proceded along the banks of the Rhine to the place of festivity, which was situaded at a small distance from the town. A tournament had been announced for that day and when anything was to be seen, the citizens of ancient Mayence, like those of the present day, were not the last to appear on such occasions.

It was a fine summer-day, which the archbishop had chosen for the feast; the sun shone brilliantly, the trees overladen with ripe fruits promised a rich harvest. The waves of the Rhine resplendent in the rays of the sun bore decorated barges filled with merry people, and splendid carriages containing ladies and cavaliers whirled clouds of dust in the air, while a long procession of foot-passengers jostled on, all bound for the place of tournament.

Numbers of all classes of society had left their homes; the soldier, exempt from duty, the scholar and the selfconceited artist: the modest, timid maiden and the loquacious matron. Merry young fellows elbowed their way through the crowd, laughing and singing, not taking care of the remarks of the disconcerted citizens, nor of the murmurs and imprecations of the soldiers.

The balustrades were filled. A crowd of beautiful ladies looked from their gallery at the knights, who had come to gain the prizes. Behind the balustrades an immense crowd of spectators could be seen thronging close together; Peals of merry laughter, jokes of all kinds and the clashing of arms as the knights moved in the lists helped to pass away the time until the arrival of the archbishop whose richly decorated pavilion was still empty. A florish of trumpets at lenght announced his arrival. Four out riders preceded the carriage, which was drawn by six horses and surrounded by young knights, wo in their splendid armour galloped at both sides of the archbishop. Then followed a long train of carriages, containing the gentlemen and ladies of the court, and the empty places in the gallery were soon occupied by them, upon which the heralds gave the signal, to begin the tournament.

From among the ladies, present to deliver the first prize, the archbishop had chosen the beautiful and virtuous Anne of Walpode, which choice was approved by every one, for she was of noble origin, lovely and amiable and fully deserved the preference. Behind her stood her father, whose dark, simple coat was decorated by the gold-chain of knighthood, his eye roved searchingly through the gay throng in the tiltyard, where the lances flew about in splinters and the sand rose in clouds from under the horses hoofs.

The hearts of the ladies beat in great excitement, for just then two cavaliers had couched their lances for the third time, and rushed upon one another at full speed; with a shock they met and as if struck by lightning one of them was thrown from his horse, while the other leapt to the ground and admist acclamations and applause offered his hand to his adversary.

The conqueror was a handsome youth and as he knelt down before Anne of Walpode, to receive the prize, unspeakable rapture shone from both their eyes. Blushingly she delivered him the prize, which he pressed tenderly to his lips.

The father took his hand, shook it warmly and presented him to the archbishop, who address'd him thus:

„You have fought valliantly, Sir John, and as I value your courage, I appoint you my chamberlain.“

„No thanks!“ said he, stopping the knight's

expressions of gratitude: „I know your desires and I congratulate on your fature. Salute your betrothed, for now you are in a position to demand her hand! Or is it otherwise?" asked he smilingly of Arnold of Walpode.

„l have always wished", replied Arnold, „to have such a valiant and honest son-in-law; but he, who lays claim to Anna's hand, must firstly prove, that he is worthy of it."

Distracted with joy and full of gratitude for this unforeseen nomination, the young man could not find words, to express his feelings and against his will he remained by the side of the patrician, although the sound of the trumpets announced the renewal of the tournament.

„Mingle with the crowd, dear John, and come and dine with me, when yon return from the castle and have got your appointment!" whispered Arnold in the ear of the young man, who warmly squeezed the hand of the noble father; then he withdrew hastily, while the patrician went smiling to his place behind his daughter, whose cheeks were covered with blushes and dared not to look at him.

It happened, that on the day of the tournament count Diether of Katzenellenbogen was likewise present at Mayence and he saw the charming daughter of the patrician. Her great fortune as well as her grace and beauty weighed

8

heavily with the count, whose purse had suffered a little by the rebuilding of the stronghold of Rheinfels. Confiding in his power and nobility, he presented himself before Arnold of Walpode, to demand the hand of his daughter, and believed, that he would think himself much honoured by this proposal.

„It is not right," replied Walpode, „that the daughter of a free town should unite herself to a Baron, who is accustomed, to regard the goods of citizens and merchants as a lawful prize. You have recently rebuilt the castle of Rheinfels, to levy custom upon the passengers and to impede the navigation and trade to and from the towns. If you think, that the town would enable you by the dowry of the bride, to make your stronghold still stronger and to fortify it better for the oppression of its inhabitants, you deceive yourself, for I shall never give my consent and still less now, as she is already bethrothed."

The count grew pale with anger and withdrew towards the door, saying savagely:

„You have appreciated my castle well: yes, it shall be henceforth a stumbling-stone for you and bring you to ruin, proud citizens!"

„Baron", exclaimed Walpode, „don't forget, that Schwarz discovered powder, with which strongholds can be destroyed."

„We shall see!" murmured Diether withdra-

wing, while Walpode retired into his arpartment.
„Yes“, said he, walking up and down, „the
feudal power must be destroyed.“ It is the duty
of the towns, to demolish the strongholds; we
have the means, to do it; we possess money and
a sufficient number of brave men, who are not
afraid of death, when the welfare of their fellow-
citizens is endangered. Singly we are exposed
to the attacks of a great number, who do us
harm and we are unable to retaliate. The power
of a single town is too weak to undertake anything against those barons and counts with hope
of success. But the allied towns can oppose
them in considerable forces, and prove their ruin.
This confederation must be the aim of our endeavours and I will do my utmost, to attain it
and to secure the welfare of my native town.“

But in spite of all the pains, which the
patrician took to persuade the towns to enter
into a confederacy, his plan was baffled by the
phlegma of those, who should have been the best
promoters of his intensions.

They thought the plan praiseworthy and patriotic; they did not reject it, but they had
doubts about its execution.

While the patrician thus took care of the
welfare of his town, the lovers passed happy
days. The young chamberlain dedicated his spare
moments to the society of his love and by this

daily intercourse the ties of love and friendship became still stronger. The wedding-day was at last fixed and the whole town rejoiced in the hope of seeing something extraordinary and brilliant; the young people were the happiest of all not on account of the brilliant festivity, but because they had attained the aim of their wishes.

The happy day at last approached and the people, who were invited to the wedding, came from near and far, to take part in the festivities. The guests were of the richest and most esteemed families; for the father of the happy couple wished to profit by this opportunity, to propose his plan to the representatives of the different towns, whom he had invited, with the intention to persuade them, to enter into a confederacy against the robbers.

The report of the approaching wedding-festivities at Mayence reached the castle of Diether, who in fury paced his room, thinking of the satirical remarks, which would be made at his expense. Hatred boiled in his heart and he cursed himself and his power for not having yet found opportunity of inflicting a considerable damage to the town of Mayence and particularly to its noblest citizen.

The hollow sound of a horn came from the tower and was re-echoed by the neigbouring mountains. „What is the matter?“ cried the count through the window.

„A troop of armed people, who bear a flag!" replied the watchman. „To horse, yeomen! They pass just in time for me to appease my rage! To horse!" was cried in the court-yard, while the count shut the window with a sardonic smile. „Ah", murmured he, „if those travellers are wedding-guests! They shall celebrate the wedding in the company of rats and mice and not with my enemies!

As peaceful, as the castle had been before, as noisy was it now. The clinking of arms the tramp of horses and the boisterous laughter of the soldiers sounded from every side.

When the knight was equipped, he descended with heayv steps into the yard, where he found his men armed for battle and after having mounted his steed and lowered his beaver, the troop rode with full speed over the bridge, towards the place, which the watchmann had indicated.

As the sentinel had announced, there were on the high-road a great number of citizens, to whom the peasants of the neighbourhood were joined, as it was necessary in those times, to travel in large numbers.

Carriages, laden with goods followed the troop; they were surrounded by some soldiers, to protect not only the merchandises, but also the women therein. The train consisted chiefly of patricians and merchants of Cologne, Bacharach

and St. Goar, who resorted to Mayence, to assist
at the wedding-festivity and according to the
practise of those times took advantage of this
opportunity, of exchanging their goods and rene-
wing their business connexions.

Among the women a young girl was especially
to be noticed, whose delicate features and charming
appearance showed she was of noble birth and
being an intimate friend of the bride could not
omit to be present at the wedding. The young
people of the train surrounded her and endeavoured
to obtain a smile or kind look.

The citizens travelled without any fear of
danger, believing to have a sufficient security in
their passports. But they were more surprised
than arlarmed, when they saw themselves surrounded by a troop of armed soldiers. The
travellers approached the leader of the troop
respektfully, who with lowered beaver and nacked
sword had followed his men, and delivered him
their passports.

„Before all!" cried he, without looking at the
passports, „wither are you going?"

„To Mayence, where the wedding of Anne
Walpode is celebrated! We are invited to assist
at the festivity."

„Is that the true object of your journey?"
asked the knight, with an ironical smile.

„Yes, Sir knight!" replied a venerable old

man, who still managed his horse with the dexterity and force of a youth.

„Then I can't help you; you must celebrate the wedding in my castle; I am in enmity with Walpode and his friends are my enemies."

After this declaration the citizens prepared to fight, but those, who on the way had joined them and had nothing to risk but their lives, had run away at the approach of the soldiers and the others after a short resistance were led as prisoners into the castle.

The travellers were expected at Mayence with impatience, but in vain; the news arrived, that they had been attacked by Diether of Katzenellenbogen out of revenge to Walpode and had been led as prisoners into his castle.

This alarming news about her friends deeply affected the bride, while it was for the energetical father a hint from heaven, to profit by this event, for the execution of his plan.

In an animated speech he showed the citizens the great want of security on the roads, by which trade was rendered very difficult, nay even impossible and the welfare of the towns much injured; he represented the miserable fate of the unhappy prisoners, who notwithstanding their passports had been killed or imprisoned; finally he knew so well how to inflame his hearers with rage, that they swore, not to rest, before they had crushed the power of the proud robbers!"

This resolution was instantly formed and all, who were present, were invited to sign. The prisoners were not forgotten. Money was collected for them and the Prim Bishops help solicited and on the third day an enthusiastic troop of soldiers marched to Rheinfels and succeeded in releasing them.

After their return, the wedding was celebrated, but it was more like a festivity after a battle, than a marriage-feast.

The league, which was here concluded, proved, that Arnold of Walpode had not exaggerated the forces of the confederate towns.

The heads of stone.

As one passes through the gate, called „Gauthor" in Mayence one sees above the military guard-house the image of the Virgin Mary, which in former times must have been held in particular veneration, for every criminal, who, on his way to the place of execution, succeeded in escaping and kneeling before this sacred image, was set at liberty.

Having passed through the gate and arrived at the outside, one can upon close examination see two stone-heads embedded in the wall to which the following tradition has reference.

In the year 1462 the archiepiscopal see of Mayence was occupied by the wise and noble Diether of Isenburg.

The elector and archbishop was detested by Pope Pius II., because he opposed the papal power. The emperor hated him likewise and both tried to dethrone him in favour of Adolph of Nassau.

A contest broke out between the two electors and as Mayence remained faithful to Diether-Adolphus approached with an army and laid siege to the town. The citizens of Mayence fought heroically. Men and women, young and old took arms, and proved themselves courages in this deplorable warfare. But Adolph's soldiers were just as excellent and he enclosed the town so, that famine and misery soon reigned in it.

At this time many fishermen and boatmen lived near the streets bordering on the Rhine, who formed a considerable company. They like all other companies took part in the war and, led by their chief, defended either the bulwarks or rowed in their frail boats along the Rhine to surprise the enemy and suddenly attack him by water. They also distinguished themselves during the famine by their fishing, although continually attacked by the enemy, who had procured boats, to attack the town from the Rhine-side and also dispute the fishing.

In a miserable cottage in the „Fisherman-street" sat one evening-the boatman Walderer, with his head leaning on his hands. A faint light threw its dismal ray over the room and exhausted itself in a corner, where his sick wife lay groaning with hunger and pain on a bed of straw. He suddenly rose and with anger pictured in his emaciated features struck the table violently with his clenched fist and exclaimed:

„This fasting is unsupportable!" I can't endure this cursed life any longer! For two days and nights I have been defending the bulwarks of the Rhine and fishing with the rest and while the fish for the elector's table are saved, ours are taken by the enemy. What is our reward? We must hunger and fight for his lordship, who feasts and revels at our charge. To say the truth, I prefer to side with Adolphus, instead of with Diether, who deals only in fine words, which are of no account.

„Our father, which art in heaven", commenced his sick wife in a hollow voice „hallowed be thy name, thy kingdome come. Thy will be done on earth, at it is in heaven. Give us this day our daily bread and forgive us our trespasses, as we forgive our trespassers, and lead us not into temptation, but deliver us from evil!"

„Amen!" concluded a youthful voice and a lovely girl rose from her seat near her mother's pillow and approched her angry father:

„Father", said she softly, „will you not take a little rest? You are weary and fatigued. I will bring you your supper and will then retire to my room."

„Let me alone! Shall I eat, while you fast and suffer? No, by all that's holy, I will not taste a bit of that, which you have spared from your mouth."

„Dear father, we do not deprive ourselves of food so much!"

„Hush, Gertrude! I feel no hunger but only rage! Don't you know, that my petition for assistance and help has been shamefully refused, and I am obliged to fight for a cowardly league of monks and priests!"

„The Lord will appear in a cloud, to separate the just from the unjust, the faithful from the unfaithful!"

„Hold your tongue wife! Is it just, to leave the poor wretch in need, and himself to live in luxury? It is just to arm citizens against citizens?"

„You must obey your sovereign!"

„Ha; ha! Does that appease our hunger? Must we not take care of ourselves first? No, by heavens! If you had not detained me, I would have deserted long before this into the camp of our enemy Adolphus, for he is our sovereign, approved of by the pope and does not let his people starve and perish!"

„God preserve us from him! He attacks our lawful sovereign!"

„That you don't understand!"

„Father, do you forget, what father Clemens said!"

To the deuce with your hypocrites and mendicant friars! They are never in want of words, he who confides in words, runs into misery. Once more I tell you, it is better, to desert to Adolphus than to remain here!"

The maiden weeping turned towards the bed of straw, but her sick mother started up in her miserable clothing, which scarce covered her meager limbs and raised menacingly her fleshless arms.

"Husband!" exclaimed she, with a woeful accent "you think of treachery! I see it coming! Woe! Woe! Do you hear? It will be your ruin!"

Saying this she sank upon her pillow.

"Mother, dear mother!" cried her girl, hastening towards her. "Holy virgin, she is dead!"

"Let her be dead; Death is preferable to famine and misery!"

"Father, Father help!"

But her father paid no attention to her, as at that moment a knock at the door called his attention to it, through which; after he had opened it, three men entered. One of them a young fishermann, hastened to salute Gertrude, who sat weeping on her bed.

The two others, wrapped in their cloacks remained at the door and looked at the boatman, who stared at one of them in surprise.

Just then the sick wife, who had only fainted, uttered a sigh and murmured: "He approaches!"

With a shout of joy the daughter hastened towards her and the fisherman, who had kneeled down, seized her thin hands and pressed them is his.

After having also affectionately pressed the hands of the girl, he turned towards the boatman and his guests and said lowly:

„When I was out to-day, to see, if I could fish something for you, Walderer, I met these two men, who promised me a reward, if I introduced them into the town!"

„You know me, Walderer!" said one of them.

„You are Heinz of Hechtsheim!"

Quite right! I have a wife in the town, the daughter of Sternberger! This man wishes to find a place of concealment and if you are inclined to give it to him, you shall not repent it!"

„If you give me a lodging!" said the other, and promise secrecy, I will pay you well; take this purse; it may do you great service!"

„Don't take it, Walderer!" cried the wife.

„Be silent!" replied the boatman. „You may take your lodging in Gertrude's room and I warrant you, nobody shall hear of it!"

Then he turned towards the young man saying: „Remain here, I will lead the strangers up stairs;

but you women", added he with a gloomy air "be quiet and hold your tongues!"

"Come!" said he to the strangers, taking the candle and guiding them up a narrow staircase to the appartment of his daughter.

"John!" said the maid, weeping, when her father was gone and it grew dark in the room, "do you know the strangers?"

"No, but your father must know them!

"They come perhaps from the camp of our enemies!"

"I thought so, Gertrude, and have therefore conducted them hither!"

"If they would betray the town!"

"Two men only? That's impossible, Gertrude?"

"Do you know that for certain?"

Quite certainly and if we don't gain the money, another does!"

"We must tell it to father Clemens!" interrupted the mother.

"Not at all!" The stranger does not want to be recognized!

"We commit perhaps a sin!"

"Where can the sin be in that? We are poor, Gertrude and miserable, We don't yet foresee the issue and it is not a sin, to gain money honestly!"

"But if they were betrayers, unhappy youth!

Can you, as a traitor, pretend to the hand of Gertrude?"

„Gertrude knows, how I love her. If the stranger is a traitor, her father will surely detect him."

„The conversation was interrupted by the return of the boatman, accompanied by Heinz.

„Gertrude, take this money and buy something strengthening for your mother. John will accompany you."

„Go, go, Gertrude! I have something to say to your father!"

The maid reluctantly took the monney and withdrew, weeping bitterly, John followed and tried to console her.

Heinz after squeezing the boatman's hand and whispering something in his ear departed, also.

„Walderer", began his wife, after the stranger's departure, „I am dying, I feel the approach of death! Who knows? Perhaps I will leave this world to night, for my mind is clear and I can see the future. Do not let the stranger corrupt you. You are discontented; poverty and distress make you angry and you murmur against Providence and its decrees. Do not bring us into infamy, Walderer. I know, that poverty is painful, but infamy is still more so. Do not think, that it will be better under Adolphus. Where God is, everthing is for the best and God is

with us, if we fulfil the duties, which we have
to perform. Promise me, not to be persuaded by
the stranger, for I forsee a great misfortune!"

„What evil can come, Anne, from granting
him a lodging?"

„He thinks of treason within our walls."

„Would to God the war would end through it."

„It will, but to our disgrace!"

„Adolphus is our lawful sovereign and it is
already disgrace enough to fight against him."

„Give to God, what is God's and to the king,
what is the king's! Diether is our sovereign and
not he."

„It is sorrowful enough, not to know, who
our sovereign is."

„God has ordained it so and we must submit!"

„And starve!"

„He can save us!"

„But he will not save us, for he abhors
these unblessed warfares! No, I have enough
of this government of Diether. Instead of reward, one gets nothing but contempt and vain
promises!"

„And your salvation?"

„I care not. If I must suffer here and starve
to gain it."

„Oh! sighed his wife, sinking down upon
her pillow." Unhappy man! You run into your
ruin!"

„By no means, friend!" interrupted the stranger, who had entered by stealth and listened to the discourse. Be faithful to Adolphus, for he is our lawful prince, the citizens have recognized him as such and detest the other!"

The boatman viewed with astonishment the warlike mien of his guest, but his wife looked with disquietude at him. The guest approached the boatman, drew him into a corner and whispered something to him.

The wife followed them anxiouly with her feverish and brilliant eyes, rose from her bed and approached them, dragging herself along on hands and feet.

The boatman, gained by the pressing words of the stranger, cried:

„I shall be yours! And confound Diether!"

His wife uttered a woeful cry and sunk down at his feet. When he stooped to raise her, she was dead.

Tears filled his eyes, when he raised the corpse of his wife from the ground and laid it on the bed. The stranger looked with emotion at the skeleton-like form of the dead woman.

„You owe that to your sovereign and his criminal treason against the emperor and the empire! Instead of bread, he has given you promises. Your wife died of hunger. You yourself are starving."

„She was a good and honest wife!"

„May she rest in pease! But now is no time to complain. When you are alone, come up stairs into my room; I have many things to tell you!"

Soon after his depature Gertrude and John returned; they wept with him and lamented her death.

The following day father Clemens came, a dominican friar, whose words were pious and religious, but whose eyes were roguish and sensual. He consoled the boatman and his daughter. He blessed the corpse and interred it.

„Gertrude!" said Walderer; as soon as this sad ceremony was finished, „I have only you remaining in the world now and when I am absent, you have no one to protect you, but yourself. Be therefore prudent and heedful in all, what you do. Be discreet and before all keep silence respecting the stranger's presence, for that would uselessly harm us."

Gertrude promised it. But she said to herself: „I may however confide it to God, and father clemens represents God in the confessional."

When the friar returned to the house of the boatman and Gertrude was alone, she confided to him her fears and sorrows regarding the hidden retreat of the stranger.

The friar reflected upon the matter. He praised the girl, he stroked her rosy cheeks carresingly and then bade her, lead him into the stranger's room. When the stranger saw the monk entering, he quickly drew his sword.

"Softly, softly noble knight!" cried the monk, at the same time withdrawing cautiously towards the door. "I come, to offer you my services and I hope, that we will agree together!"

The monk remained with the stranger a long time. Before his departure he stroked the cheeks of the girl once more, saying:

"Farewell, my dear and do not grieve too much over your mother's death. She is gone to heaven and for her soul's repose you may say five pater nosters in the chapel of the Holy Ghost."

"But how can I come thither, reverend father?"

"Oh, if you like, I will take you to the chapel."

"I am afraid, that my father will disapprove of it."

"Who wishes to pray, wants no permission for it. Besides, do, as you like and concerning the stranger, keep everything secret!"

He departed with a self-satisfied smile and returned after an hour with a monk's habit, which the stranger assumed and walked in this disguise through the town.

There was misery in the highest degree, to be seen. Halfstarved men and women were lying about in the streets; the typhus raged and in the corners of the streets lay decomposed corpses, which infected the air with their putrefaction. Despair and dejection reigned everywhere. The stranger examined all attentively and then went to the arithmetician Sternberger, with whom he remained a long time. At last he, the monk, Heinz and Sternberger came out together and repaired to the mayor Dudo, who in the capacity of architect had the keys of the town gates.

In the evening he returned to his retreat. The boatman had likewise just returned and reproached his daughter most violently on account of her indiscretion. The stranger quieted him and led him into his apartment.

„Walderer“, he began, „I have to day by the assistance of the monk, whom I bribed, walked through the town and have found, that all is ripe for the execution of our plan, which I will confide to you, if you are willing to serve me.“

Saying this, he untied his money-belt and poured its contents upon the table.

The boatman seized the treasure greedily, at the view of which all doubts vanished and he swore the oath of allegiance.

„You shall have twice as much, if you are faithful. Now hear, what you have to do. To night you must lead me out of the town and to morrow morning be ready, to smuggle me, and some companions in and hide us in your house."

„That is no easy matter, Sir!"

„I know it and for that reason you shall have a still greater reward. I have friends in the town, but I cannot confide in them alone and I must have security for everything. You know the by-ways of the Rhine and can smuggle me out."

„Certainly, for I am acquainted with every nook and corner of the Rhine. John will lead you to the river by a canal. I will try to be intrusted with the guard of the Gau-gate. John and myself hope to be able to let you in!"

„Very well, get me away from here; John will guide and I shall return to morrow at the same hour."

„I shall be ready, but I must see John before, who must assist me, as I cannot do everything alone!"

„Is he safe?"

„If he has given his word, he is sure and may be relied upon."

„Try to get him to consent. He shall have a fine wedding-present."

The boatman withdrew, but not without having put the money into his bag. John, seduced by the hope of marriage and the wedding-present, joined with the boatman and led the stranger by the same canal, which in later times served the Frenchmen as a passage for contraband-goods.

Gertrude uttered a light sigh, when the stranger departed. She had been tormented by the fear, that he might be discovered or her father suspected by his mysterious presence. With his depature she imagined all danger removed and now for the first time she rejoiced at having the money, acquired as she thought honestly and so easily.

However during the day she was roused from her joyful humour. The monk waited the moment when her father and lover were not at home, for the purpose of making equivocal proposition to the girl, who until then had confided in his honesty.

When Gertrude perceived his intentions and turned away with aversion, he threatened to ruin her father, for lodging the treacherous stranger and being guilty of treason to the town.

The maiden, full of alarm, fell upon her knees and implored him with tears not to do so. But the tears heightened her beauty still more; the voluptuous monk stooped, to embrace and kiss her. As she resisted, a struggle ensued, which inflamed the lust of the licentious fellow still more. Subdued by the fear of her father's ruin and still more by the violence of the impertinent wretch, the unhappy girl would have been overcome, if John at this moment had not arrived just in time to rush furiously on the monk. A struggle ensued. The maid clung desperately to her lover and prevented him killing the monk with his clasp-knife.

The boatman just then arrived and separated the two.

Father Clemens again resumed the air of the humble and devout monk, what he usually seemed to be through his hipocrisy. John briefly related what he had seen; his intention, to unmask the deceitful monk, was counteracted by Gertrude, who frightened by the threatening looks of the friar denied all.

„It is evident," said the boatman, that you did not come hither with good intentions and as we must render you harmless, you shall remain here to day as our prisoner. The reply of the monk was not listened to. Still terrified by the fisherman's knife he suffered himself to be locked up in a small room built in the town wall against which the house stood. The boatman then deliberated with John, Gertrude was sent to her room, with orders not to leave it. The rest of the day passed quietly. Walderer mounted guard that evening at the Rhine and John succeeded in leading the warriors, disguised as monks, into the town. Silently and hidden by the shadow of the narrow street, they entered the boatman's house and gathered with respectful silence around the stranger.

„Vassals“, began the latter, „we at lenght have a footing in the treacherous town and I swear, not to leave it, before I have punished the citizens and destroyed the enemy's power. Swear, to fight valiantly and then we shall, with God's help and by the triumph of this day dissolve the allegiance of the arrogant citizens, who dare to fight against us.“

„We swear!“ muttered they in a low tone at the same time, drawing their swords, the noise of which echoed hollowly through the miserable house. Walderer and John fell upon their knees.

„My lord!“ stammered the first.

Adolphus turned towards them. „You shall have your reward. Walderer, lead us to the „Gauthor“, for there my troops can with greater ease enter and commence the attack!“

It was a curious picture, to see the prince and his followers standing in their armour in the humble cottage while the boatman and John bowed humbly before them.

The feeble, glimmering light of the candle

reflected them upon the damp walls of the apartment.

At lenght the bell tolled midnight and all marched silently towards the „Gauthor“ winding their way through small, solitary streets. A gloom, which seemed to forebode evil, lay over the town and the Rhine.

Gertrude, who had still remained in her room, perceived the strange stir in the house. She crept softly down stair and lissened, holding her breath. She was convinced, that her father and John had betrayed the town; she fell upon her knees and invoked God's help.

When the men were gone, she hastened to the place, where the monk was shut up and said to him with a low voice and in haste:

„Go with me and lead me to the elector and I will forgive you all.“

„Oh, lovely maid,“ cried he ironically: „Will you side with the elector?“

„For God's sake, come! Every moment of delay endangers the town.“

A diabolical glance flashed in the eyes of the monk.

„Where is your father?“ asked he.

„Don't ask! He is gone! Woe to us! he is gone!“

„Gone? But what is it you want?“

„The enemy is in the town! Do you still hesitate?"

„Ah, pretty charmer, do you think, that I would run with you through the town and spread this news from house to house? Adolphus promised me a rich abbey, it I kept it secret and you must do so likewise and pass this night in my company; resistance is useless.

Actuated by lust he had already thrown his arms around the girl and tore the neckcloth from her bosom, while his lips approached hers. But the girl, to whom despair gave supernatural strenght, freed herself and flew like lightning from the house.

„Citizens! To arms! To arms! The enemy! The enemy!"

In this manner she ran through the streets to the house of the master of the watermans company. She knocked at the door so violently, that she awakened all the neighbours.

„What 's the matter?" asked the master.

„To arms! The enemy is in the town! To arms!"

„God forbid!" cried the old man alarmed and bidding the girl to enter.

With few words she told him, what had happened, trying as much as possible to spare her father and to make him believe her guilty of the treason. The chief guessed the truth, and prepared himself for defence

Then he quickly descended, awoke the boat-men und fishermen and ordered them to ring the alarm-bells.

During this interval, the enemy had advanced to the „Gauthor", where the guard had partly by weariness and partly by despair fallen asleep. Only the gigantic Waibel with some fellow-drink-ers, who were hot with wine and sitting round a large cup, spoke in his terms against the enemy. Suddenly Adolphus with his soldiers entered, accompanied by the mayor Dudo and while they bound the astonished Waibel and his companions, the traitor opened the sally-port. The enemy had advanced from the other side of the Rhine through the „Gartenfeld" to the „Gau-thor". There were 1600 horse and 3400 foot-soldiers under the command of Ludwig of Veldenz, Eberhard of Königstein and Alwich Sulz. They stood before the wall and had not the courage to scale it, because they saw an owl, sitting on it, which they mistook in the darkness for a sentinel. Frightened by the noise, which the soldiers made, it flew away and then the army approached and penetrated into the town through the open gate.

But here the stir was also general, the alarm-bells rang, the citizens had armed themselves and hurried through the streets, excited by rage and despair.

They all assembled. „Where is the enemy?" was asked everywhere. The women cried, the children skrieked and the confusion increased more and more.

„To the „Gauthor!" To the „Gauthor!" The enemy has entered! On, on to the „Gauthor!" and the whole mob crowded to the Gaugate, where the enemy was already engaged in close combat with the inhabitants there.

A horrible struggle ensued and the enemy could only advance step by step. Every house was a fortress. The women and girls participated in the combat, throwing pieces of furniture and firebrands from the windows. The besiegers were obliged to kill them and to set fire to the houses, for the purpose of preventing them from fighting and to secure their conquest. Volumes of smoke and flames rose into the air, which resounded with the furious cries of the combatants and the tolling of the alarm-bells.

Gertrude marched on at the head of a troop of citizens; pierced by the enemy's lances she sunk down at the feet of her horrified father and the enemy continued the bloody fight over her corpse.

The ruined and desolated town offered a pitiful sight; the citizens appeared with anxiety at the enemy's summons. Terrible were the sentences of Adolphus. All men who had been found armed were exiled and nothing was granted to them but life.

Mayence was conquered and its pride humbled. But the traitors did not escape the punishment of their conscience and the justice of God was particularly visible in the fate of Walderer and John.

The first became mad and the other threw himself with Gertrude's corpse into the Rhine.

In remembrance of this treason two heads carved in stone were inserted in the town-wall; and the small side-gate, by which the enemy had entered, was walled up.

Ingelheim.

elow Mayence, about a mile distant from the Rhine, is situated „Nieder-ingelheim" and a little farther off „Oberingelheim".

The space between these two villages must in former times have been covered with buildings and the whole named „Ingelheim".

At Ingelheim the emperor Charles the Great had a palace, which was his favourite residence. Some of its ruins still exist.

This great monarch heard one day, that a hermit lived in the Rheingau, whose wisdom was praised and talked of by all.

He cured diseases of the mind as well, as of the body and all patients, who visited his cell, besides good advice received a present such as his means permitted him to give.

The emperor, anxious to become acquainted with the hermit, despatched a messenger to him, but who to the greatest surprice of Charles brought back a message, that the hermit had declared, it was not his duty, to visit the palaces of the great, but the cottages of the poor and if the emperor wished to make his acquaintance, he might come to him, for he had more conveniences for travelling than himself.

At first Charles frowned and grew angry, then, repeating once more the hermit's reply, he could not help laughing and resolved to pay him a visit. He was curious to see the man who dared to defy him.

The more he thought about it the more he wished to have an adventure and resolved to dress in plain armour and take another name.

One night he mediated more than usual upon his plan and could not sleep; he arose in a strange excitement, put on common armour and said smilingly:

„Now for it, for I see well, that I shall find no rest, till I have satisfied my curiosity.“

Unobserved by anybody, he went to the stable, saddled a horse and left his palace without meeting a soul.

Not far from the palace was a dark forest, into which he entered. It seemed to him, as if he heard the trot of a horse. He prepared his arms, looked about and perceived a horseman, who came towards him.

When they came together, the rider who

wore black armour cried to the emperor: „Where do you come from? Where are you going?"

„I come from Ingelheim for an adventure!" replied the emperor, anxious to know how this would end.

„But why so late and alone? This is not the manner of travelling for knights who have the protection of the law."

„Ah, ah! thaught Charles to himself, „I understand, that shows he is not unter the protection of the law!" and then said aloud: And if it were so, what objection have you to it!"

„None; I would even rejoice, for then we would be companions in misfortune. What is your name?"

„My name is Charles, and yours?"

„Elbegast!"

„What? You are that Elbegast, the robber whom the emperor has sentenced?"

„Softly, my friend, softly! You speak, as if you knew nothing about robbing, I was a poor devil, the priests robbed me of my inheritance; an audacious prelate had the impudence to ridicule me and to steal from under my nose a rich consignement. By heavens, the emperor himself would not have liked it. I laid hand upon it and rescued a part of my goods. These false scoundrels who surround the emperor misinformed

10

him of the case and he sentenced me; but truly, if I were lucky enough to meet him here like you, I would tell him frankly, with what rascals and thieves he deals and I would unmask their fraud and roguery."

„Oh, friend Elbegast, you speak, like an orator."

„I speak frankly and sincerely; but enough of this. Will you ride this night with me? I have tracked something and if it is, as I believe it to be, I shall break the necks of some rascals to night, even if the emperor would hang me for it, which would, by the way be unjust."

„Perhaps you would wish him to be grateful to you and welcome you in a friendly manner on account of your skill in breaking necks."

„He ought to do so, for if I break necks to night, I do it for his benefit."

„That would be something."

„Come along with me, for I want a courageous and resolute companion."

„Onwards, Elbegast, I shall follow; only promise me, not to draw the sword without my consent."

„Well, then, forward!"

„The emperor and the robber travelled together through the forest like two friends. Elbegast guided his horse by narrow paths to a fortress hidden in the forest, made a sign to his companion to alight and follow him noiselessly.

Passing through a shrubbery they arrived at a small door, which Elbegast opened with a false key and led his companion into a small and gloomy corridor, at the end of which was a dark apartment, which was only separated by an immense folding-door from a very brilliantly lighted one. The two adventurers approached the door cautiously and listened.

They now heard a voice, speaking against the great power of the emperor, which soon would destroy the nobility, the knighthood and clergy, if they did not put a stop to it.

„To the devil with you all!" murmured Charles, peeping through an aperture, which permitted him, to get a sight of the speaker. How great was his surprise, when he recognized the count Eggerich of Eggermonde, upon whom he had heaped benefits and who was even connected by marriage with him.

„What would Charles give, if he could hear all this!" whispered Elbegast to the emperor.

„Hush! Be silent!" said Charles, squeezing his hand gratefully.

„Let us listen a little!"

And they listened again, and heard how they had fixed upon a plan of assassinating the emperor, after which all who were present took the oath upon a crucifix, which the high prelate held.

„Shall we not break the priest's neck?" whispered Elbegast angrily; „he is the same who stole my inheritance and who has brought dishonour upon me and the sentence of the emperor. Does he not merit punishment?"

„Be quiet, friend; justice shall be done to you!" replied Charles whispering and they retired, as they had come."

„Elbegast", began Charles, when they were outside, „you have rendered the emperor a service, which he will never forget; come to morrow to his palace and tell him, what you have heard; I shall be present as witness."

„Oh, that would be a nice thing", replied Elbegast smiling, „they would break my neck long before I had found an opportunity of speaking to the emperor."

„Is then the justice of the emperor so bad?" asked Charles.

„Not his, but the justice of his vassals, who commit many injustices under his name. If they got information of my denunciation of them, they would cut my throat before the emperor had heard of my arrest."

„Well then, I will speak to the emperor

myself; tell me only, where I can meet you to morrow.

„That I might be caught. Oh, Elbegast is too prudent for that! I was willing to break the rebel's skull, but you forbade it."

„Elbegast, I summon you, in the emperor's name, to appear to morrow in the palace and accuse the rascals, whom we overheard."

„And who are you who dare to summon me in the name of the emperor?" asked Elbegast alarmed.

„Your enemy before but now your friend. It is the emperor himself, who speaks to you."

At the same moment the moon appeared from behind the clouds, which had hidden it and shone full upon the manly form of the speaker, whose features were half serious and half friendly.

„My emperor and master!" cried Elbegast leaping from his horse and trembling with joy and emotion.

„You rendered me a service, when I was your enemy. Now prove me your friendship and come to the palace, as I demanded! I will prepare everything for your reception."

Saying this, he spurred his horse and returned to Ingelheim, leaving Elbegast with strange feelings moving his heart.

The sentence, which the emperor passed against the traitors, was terrible. Their punishment was not restricted to banishment and the seizure of their goods; they were publicly hanged.

Quite the contrary with Elbegast, who had come in conformity with the emperor's summons; honours and riches were heaped upon him and he remained the intimate friend of his once unknown companion in adventure.

*   *   *

In later times the emperor remembered, that in the night, so eventful for him and Elbegast he had been on the way to the hermit's cell and he once more resolved to go thither.

As he had learnt, how useful it is for a sovereign, from time to time to disguise himself and listen to the voices of his subjects, which he otherwise could not hear, he persuaded Elbegast to accompany him to the hermit's cell.

Both dressed plainly mounted on horseback and not telling any body the aim of their journey rode towards the hermitage.

Not far off from there they met a charming girl, the daughter of a charcoal-burner, who was going to market with eggs and butter. She came towards them, merrily singing.

The emperor was, as is well known very fond of the fair sex and he could not forbear to ask the young creature, whence she came and whither she was going and while she replied to his question, she looked up at him with such a childish, innocent air, that he tenderly stroked her cheeks.

The girl blushed and unluckily this blushing became her so well, that Charles bent down from his horse, seized her round the waist and tried to kiss her.

The girl glided out of his arms, and a lean man with a noble and venerable figure, behind whom the little one had taken refuge, stepped forth and adressed the emperor:

„Friend, are you married and have you daughters?"

„Suppose, I had!" replied Charles humorously.

„Well, then don't forget, what you did to this girl and censure not others more severely, than yourself, if the same should happen to your daughters.

„Elbegast", said Charles to his companion, who was laughing, „this attire is fatal to me. Fverytime, I put it on, I receive good lessons."

„And I know, from experience," replied Elbegast with a look of deep veneration, „that these lessons fall upon a productive ground."

Charles returned to Ingelheim without having been recognized; but a rich present soon made known to the old man and daughter, who the two persons were whom they met on the road.

———

Eginhard and Emma.

Emperor Charles had arranged it in his palace so that he could from a gallery of his bed-room overlook the court-yard and particularly all the entrances of the palace. Often when sleep forsook him, he arose, went to the gallery and watched, if he could discover secrets, from which he could derive pleasure or profit.

One night when looking down from the gallery, he with pleasure perceived tracks of game, in the court-yard which was covered with snow, for he was very fond of hunting. Suddenly a window in the female's apartments was opened and a head appeared for a moment, but started back as if with horror and then closed it quickly. The emperor frowned angrily and wished to know the meaning of this strange apparition, when in the same moment another head peeped forth and withdrew slowly. Charles was not left long in doubt who those persons were. A female figure alighted from the window, took a man upon her shoulders and carried him through the yard. The pale moon-light shone upon the strange pair and Charles recognized his daughter Emma, who carried her lover Eginhard, the private secretary and favourite of the emperor, in order that the track of his steps in the snow might not betray him.

Passion was the first feeling that this romantic sight stirred in Charles' breast. If he had yielded to it, he would have punished both most severely and particularly Eginhard, even with death; but when the first excitement was over, he pitied them. Besides he could not forbear laughing at the cunningness of his daughter and remembered the hermit's admonition: „Don't judge more severely, if a like thing happened to your daughters!" In deep thought he walked to and fro in his apartment, reflecting upon what he should do. The next day he bade Eginhard appear before him.

„Eginhard!" began the emperor, „last night I had a strange thought and I leave it to your wisdom to decide the case."

„My lord and emperor!" replied Eginhard, „I shall try to pronounce a sentence as just as possible."

„Well then", continued Charles, suppose somebody had heaped favours and benefits upon a

young man; and as a return for this he seduced
the daughter of his benefactor. What punishment
would this treacherous fellow deserve?

Eginhard stood pale and trembling before his
terrible judge, in whose hands was life, honour
and death. But it vexed him, to be called a
seducer, for his love to Emma was pure and
had taken deep root in his heart. He replied
therefore proudly :

„Death, if the father, cannot pardon his love!“

The emperor looked firmly at him, then he
became friendly and asked:

„Then you love my daughter? Heigh? Pro-
bably, because she is the emperor's daughter? Is
it not so? I know the sincerity of the love of
you courtiers?“

„I would love Emma, even if she were one
of the lowest born!“

„And Emma!“

„She loves me as tenderly and sincerely as
I love her!“

„Come with me!“ said Charles and betook
himself to the apartment of his surprised and
frightened daughter.

„Girl,“ said he severely, „how is it, that you
have love-intrigues behind my back and without
my knowledge? Do you know, that your seducer
must die ?“

Emma fell trembling and in a flood of tears

upon her knees and implored her father for mercy, not for her, but for Eginhard, whom she esteemed more, than all other cavalliers.

„Well said Charles at last with emotion, „you love one another and you shall be united but not remain at Ingelheim any longer; I must never see you again. You, Emma, must forget, that the emperor is your father and you, Eginhard, know, that your wife has ceased to be my daughter and has lost all claims to her dowry.“

Both kneeled down in deep emotion and begged his blessing.

„You shall have it, children, for that is the only inheritance, which I give you; farewell!“

He turned hastily back, to conceal his emotion. Eginhard and Emma departed from the palace and passed over the Rhine, to lead far from the court a quiet and humble life.

It happened in later times, that Charles lost his way in the Odenwald and came to a pretty cottage, which peeped charmingly through green trees and fragrant flowers. He entered the cottage to claim hospitality. A young wife with a lovely child upon her knees, who between strugling and laughing was trying to catch a plaything, which the mother always withdrew from its little hands, was sitting in a clean room with little but very tastefully arranged furniture.

The emperor, whose arrival had not disturbed

the pretty young mother, who was happy in playing with her child, stood lingering at the door,
surprised at the view of such pure domestic
happiness and a tear stole from his eye, when
he recognized in this happy mother Emma, who
now made aware of the emperor's presence by
her child, who was staring at the stranger, had
no sooner seen her father, than she rose hastily
and pressing her child to her bosom approached
him trembling and weeping.

„Where is Eginhard?“ asked the emperor
softly.

He is tilling the ground for our maintenance!“
stammer'd Emma, looking anxiously at her father,
to see, if he was angry or not. But as she
perceived, that his eyes were filled with tears,
she could not restrain herself any longer and
ran to him and fell at his feet, showing him
her child.

„Father“, said she sobbing, „look at your
grand-son and bless him, that he may become
by this blessing as happy, as his parents.“

The emperor took the child tenderly in his
arms, kissed it and pressed Emma to his bosom,
saying:

Truly, you have well understood the happiness of submission, I have reason to envy you;
but enough of tears, let us think of the reality,
for I am fatigued and hungry.“

Emma went to the kitchen and prepared the supper; she was well aquainted with cookery and knew how to prepare the venison so nicely, that Charles relished it only when cooked by his daughter.

Eginhard soon came home; his face was sunburnt, but his features expressive of contentment and happiness: he was astonished at the sight of the emperor and heard with gratitude, that he had blessed the child.

The evening passed away merrily, the emperor was very contented and in the best humour. When his train arrived; he presented Eginhard to them as the lawful husband of his daughter and nominated him instantly counsellor of state.

The happy pair returned to Ingelheim in triumph and often visited the humble cottage, in which they had passed so many happy hours, to repose from the troubles and cares of the court.

Adolfseck.

e insert a tradition here, which, though not quite historical, yet gives a charming picture of the romantic middle-age, in which love and bravery formed a contrast so highly interesting.

A war broke out between France and Germany, because the French kings, could not withstand meddling in the domestic affairs of the German empire.

The bishop of Strasburg, who concluded a treacherous league with the French, challenged the emperor of Germany; Adolphus of Nassau entered Alsace with an army, to meet the enemy's troops and punish the traitors.

Adolphus was an excellent commander. He fought valiantly in the first ranks of his army. But when his sharp eyes discovered a blunder in the enemy's lines he immediately exchanged his sword for the commander's staff and led his soldiers against the weak point. His ardour

in fighting and his warlike spirit often led him
beyond the bound of caution and advancing too
far he was often wounded and carried from the
field of battle by his friends. That was also the
case in Alsace, where he was borne into a convent to have his wounds healed. He had for
his nurse a young novice, by name Imagina, a
charming maid, who performed this duty with
an unwearied patience and the most generous
resignation.

When she was near him, the Duke felt an
unutterable calm in his soul, his wounds seemed
to heal as if by enchantment: but in his heart
another wound opened, and one day, not being
able to master his emotion, he seized her hand
and confessed to her, that her divine features
and noble disposition had inflamed his heart with
ardent love for her.

The young girl blushed and grew pale alternately at hearing the monarch's declaration. Tears
started to her eyes and rolled down her cheeks
like pearls, as his words re-echoed in her heart.
She withdrew her hand gently and retired, but
when the hour arrived, at which she usually
repaired to the patient, she did not return she
had announced herself sick which was really
true.

Three days and three painful nights passed
away, during which the emperor had not seen

her and tormented by impatience and perhaps by repentance of his rash declaration, he tossed about in his bed and found no rest. The third night the door opened noiselessly and Imagina entered, pale and disturbed, but beautiful as he had never seen her before.

„Fly, prince,“ cried she quickly; „the bishop of Strasburg is about to take you prisoner and you have not a moment to loose.“

The emperor rose hastily, called his servant, who slept in the adjoining room and sent him to the commander of the troops; and he, accompanied by the novice, walked through the corridors of the convent, which resounded hollowly, then through the church, till he arrived at a small door, the key of which the novice had procured.

„God and the holy Virgin be praised“, said she sighing, „that you are saved! Farewell, noble and generous prince! Do not forget me?“

Saying so she was about to retire to the convent, but the emperor, who had been fascinated during his sickness by the image of the charming maid, begged her not to abandon him and instead of returning to her cell, to go with him as his wife.

The lovely maid could not resist, but followed her lover. Wrapped in a cloack and protected

11

by the night's darkness they arrived at the banks of the Rhine, which they crossed in a ferry.

The emperor, rescued by the care of the young novice from the craft of the priesthood, led his army against the enemy again, and after some successes consented to conclude peace with France.

After the conclusion of peace he led his lovely deliverer into his states of Nassau and at Eichthal near Schwalbach built the castle of Adolphseck, which he destined for her residence.

He passed many happy days there at the side of his charming Imagina. But at lenght the political horizon became clouded by the intrigues of his own cousin, the archbishop of Mayence, who made an alliance with other princess of the realm and declared Albert of Austria co-emperor, by which Adolphus was compelled to combat for his crown.

At Göllheim, not far from the „Donnersberg", the two armies met: the combat was fierce and Adolphus, hurried away by his ardour in fighting, forgot, his commander's duty, advanced too far and fell, pierced by a lance from an attack of cavalry. The army, bereft of its commander, became confused and fled. Albrecht triumphed and became emperor of Germany. Imagina had followed Adolphus at a distance and waited in the convent of Rosenthal for the issue of the

battle and her husband's return. She had listened
in the evening to the war-cry, resounding from
afar and a sad, gloomy foreboding moved her
heart, when she found that her consort did not
return with the coming night.

Pale and distracted she went to the field of
battle, which was illumined by the silver rays of
the moon. After she had sought a long time,
she suddenly heard a noise in the bushes, and
the Prince's faithful grey-hound ran to her; whining and pulling at her dress, he made her follow
him through hedges of thorn and thistles and
over fields. The faithful animal led her to the
place, where the corpse of the emperor laid;
weeping she approached it and wiped off the
blood which covered his temples and lips. Soldiers
passing by, assisted her in transporting the killed
emperor to the convent, where he was interred.
Imagina took the veil at Rosenthal and soon
followed her beloved Adolphus into another world.

The castle of Adolphseck was destroyed by
Albrecht, who however ordered a cross to be
erected on the place, where the emperor died.

Eppenstein.

In a charming valley of the Taunus mountains are to be seen the ruins of the castle of Eppenstein, whose lords are renowned in the history of the Rheingau and of all Germany*).

We give the following legend of the castle's foundation.

Knight Eppo, while one day eagerly pursuing a wild boar, lost his way in the forest. Vainly he sounded the buggle; nobody replied but the echo which seemed to mock him.

Discouraged and fatigued he alighted to repose; but he soon started up filled with admiration and rapture at hearing a soft, charming melody out of the dephts of the forest; it was sung by a pure and expressive voice. The count Eppo having cut a passage through the thicket with his sword, arrived at the entrance of a grotto

---

*) The nobles of Eppenstein were very rich and five of them occupied the archiepiscopal see of Mayence.

where he saw a maid with eyes uplifted to heaven, singing a sacred melody. Eppo stopped
with ecstasy at this view, but the young girl,
who saw him, began to weep and implored his
protection. She told him, that a giant had taken
her and brought her hither, that he had fallen
into a deep sleep, but not without having previously tied her to a rock, lest she should escape him.

„Well then, how shall I help you?" exclaimed Eppo impatient and anxious.

„Return to my castle and get the consecrated
net, which I have kept there; I will cover him
with that net in the name of the holy Trinity
and then he will not be able to move and be
as weak as a child."

The count did, as she had told him, conveyed
the net to the grotto and hid himself to await
the issue. When the giant had left the grotto
and went to the other side of the mountain to
cut a reed for a pipe, the maid took the net,
ran to the summit of the mountain and laid the
net down which she strewed with leaves, moss
and fragrant herbs.

The giant perceived with satisfaction her
activity and when she had finished, she bade him
lay down to try, if it was comfortable. The giant
readily consented to her request and stretched
himself upon it. The young woman threw the

net instantly over him in the holy Trinity's name
and ran away, frightened by the horrible howling of her prisoner. She wanted the knight to
depart directly with her, but he bade her wait
a little; he ran towards the mountain and pushed
the giant, who tried vainly to free himself, down
the precipice, where cursing and howling he
was dashed to pieces.

The free'd maid became the knight's wife.
The castle Eppenstein was built on the place,
where they had first seen each other and the
giant's bones are still shown there, to attest the
truth of the tale.

Falkenstein.

On the road to Homburg on the summit of a rocky mountain are to be seen the ruins of the castle of Falkenstein. A zigzag path leads up to the castle. The following is reported about the origin of this road.

Once there must have lived a maid of wonderful beauty, whose head-strong and brutal father turned away all people, who climbed up the stony and steep path, to view this lovely creature.

Among the visitors where frequently to be seen noblemen, who wished to court the beauty, but the coarse reception of the father after having climbed up the rugged path only to receive coldness from his daughter in spite of the enthusiastic homages which they paid to her, detained them from coming again. There was only Kuno of Sayn whom the difficulty of the way and the gloomy looks of the old knight did not withhold from climbing up the mountain, for he was the only one who received the kind looks of the charming maid.

In the evening, when he stood with her on the terrace and admired the sunset, when he drew her attention to the beauties of the surrounding scenery and explained to her the situation of his castle, their hands met tenderly and the young girl dit not withhold her rosy lips from the sweet kisses of her lover.

He climbed up to the castle one day, but the way was bitter and tiresome work, he wiped away the hot perspiration from his fore-head, as the heat was suffocating and his heart was already inflamed by a fire, which made the blood flow quicker through his vains. He was resolved to make known to the father his intention of marrying the daughter, but when he thought of the knight's roughness, his heart failed him.

After having reposed a little at the entrance of the castle, the knight resolutely ascended the winding staircase of the tower, behind whose window's curtains his mistress watched for his return with violent throbbing of the heart.

The lord of Falkenstein had seen the toilsome journey of the climber, from a small bow-window of his apartment and asked:

„For what purpose have you come hither?"

„I declare to you frankly, noble lord", replied the young man, looking passionately at the girl who withdrew blushing, „that I love your charming daughter and I am come to ask for the maid's hand."

Falkenstein listened to the proposition, knitting his brows and walking up and down his room his hands folded behind him. After having reflected thus a long time, he stopped suddenly and said: „Sir knight, if I were come into a castle to woo the owner's daughter, I had praised the ruggedness of the way, instead of blaming it; but that's the world's course; the morals become worse from day to day and the young people now are not like those of former times! Oh! those times were golden; hm!"

„But, Sir knight", said the young man, „I am conscious of no blunder! I ascended the mountain cheerfully and would have done so, if the way had been twice as steep!"

„Yes, yes! I know you cavaliers!" replied Falkenstein, nodding. „Well, you shall have my daughter, upon the condition, that you have made by to morrow morning the way, leading up to the castle, practicable for horsemen and carriages!"

„But that's impossible!" exclaimed the knight frightened. „Hundreds of miners could not finish it in a month!"

„Perform it as well as you can!"

Dejected and without having again seen his

love, the young man left the castle and racked
his brains in vain, reflecting how he could conquer the old knight's obstinacy. Nothing occured
to his thoughts and when he contemplated the
rock, on which the castle stood, he shuddered,
for he was persuaded, that he could never accomplish the extravagant wish of the stubborn old
man. He felt himself woefully dejected at the
thought of being obliged to resign for ever the
being he loved, and when he perceived her on
the plattform, waving her handkerchief; he withdrew hastily, saying to himself: „No, I will try
my utmost, before I renounce her!"

He returned in full speed to his castle, summoned the surveyor of his mines, who had opened
a mine for him, from which he got copper and
silver and explained to him what he wished; the
surveyor declared, shrugging his shoulders, that
it was impossible for him, to make the road
even if he employed all the miners, working day
and night for months.

The knight had already expected that; he
retired, uttering a deep sigh and strayed into
the depths of the shadowy forest, to give vent
to his grief. He walked through bushes and
thorns; sometimes he opened a passage for himself with his sword, now he ran like a mad-man,
then he stopped at once sighing and looking
indifferently at the flowing off a rivulet, which

winded its way through moss and fragrant wood-
herbs. But nothing could divert the knight, for
as his mind was gloomy, all nature appeared
gloomy to him. Night threw her shadows over
the forest and the knight growing more melancholy
bewailed the loss of his love with tears in his
eyes and cursed the obstinacy of her father.

Suddenly there stood before him an old man
with a long white beard down to his belt, clad
in a grey gown with large sleeves.

„Young man,“ began he, „if you promise me,
to order your miners, to dig before noon and not
after, I will assist you and lead you into the
arms of your bride.“

The young man stared at first with astonishment at the old man, but as he had often heard
of sprights, haunting the mountains and that
they were kind humane beings who liked to be
charitable, especially, if people behaved nobly,
replied:

„If you can help me, I shall grant you everything, that you demand: for no price is too high,
at wich I may attain my happiness.

„Well then,“ said the little man, dissappear-
ing, „ride to-morrow on horseback to Falkenstein, ask once more for the daughter's hand and
you will obtain it.

Hovering between hope and doubt he returned
home and could not close his eyes the whole

night. With sun rise the next day he ordered his horse to be saddled and rode in all haste to the castle, up the broad zigzag-path which had appeared there during the night. Having entered the castle to the merry sounds of the horn and shouts of joy; he cried:

„Rise, lord of Falkenstein! Open your eyes. The way is finished and your daughter mine!"

Pale and with tears of joy the daughter descended the winding-stairs and sunk on her lover's breast. The father followed, alarmed at the last night's events, by which his obstinacy had become completely broken.

The knight, still confounded by that, which had happened, told his meeting with the spright and was informed, that in the night a terrible thunderstorm had raged over Falkenstein and that in the intervals the strokes of hatchets had been heard mingled with loud loughter; the noise approached nearer and nearer; until it arrived at the entrance of the castle, when it suddenly ceased.

Seized by terror, they had risen and passed the night in prayers. With day-break they had laid themselves down and slumbered, when suddenly roused by the sounds of his horn and the trampling of his horse they awoke. The old man gave his son-in-law the advice never to be as obstinate, as he had been himself.

The tradition does not tell us, if the young husband followed the advice. But the wonderful road is still to be seen and when we reflect upon the exertion, which was necessary to finish it, it does not seem improbable, that the mountain-sprites assisted in the work.

————

Mouse-tower.

ike a silver-thread flows the Rhine above Bingen and on its vine-covered banks towns, villages and country-seats are scattered about, which form a most picturesque and beautiful sight. But below Bingen it rushes furiously on through the hills and dashes against the rocks, that stand in its way, as if they wished to stop its headlong speed. At the entrance of this beautiful valley, just between the smooth-quiet, and the strong and foaming part of the river stands on a small island a tower called the „Mouse-tower". The following tradition explains the origin of its name.

Hatto, archbishop of Mayence is said to have kept a well-filled barn locked up, during a famine and by his good living and plenty had excited the starving people to revolt. The prelate gave orders. to seize the rebels, to shut them up in a barn and then to set fire to it. Not content with this diabolical order he added to it insult, by comparing the lamentations of the poor sufferers to the squeaking of mice.

In the night, which followed this atrocious deed, mice penetrated into the archbishop's palace, and were about to tear the flesh from off his bones. Hatto fled, crossed the Rhine and suspended his bed in the tower, but in vain: the mice followed him and made him die a lingering and horrible death.

It is strange, that history represents Hatto in a quite different light to what tradition does. The first says, that he was a wise and learned, but also an ambitious prelate. Cuning, enterprizing and proud, but not very scrupulous in the choice of the means to arrive at his aim; he had many enemies as well among the nobility, as among the people. This hatred most likely gave rise to the horrible tradition.

* * *

The Tradition of Bishop Hatto.

The summer and autumn had been so wet,
That in winter the corn was growing yet,
'T was a piteous sight to see all around
The grain lie rotting on the ground.

Every day the starving poor
Crowded around Bishop Hatto's door,
For he had a plentiful last year's store,
And all the neighbourhood could tell,
His granaries were furnish'd well.

At last Bishop Hatto appointed a day
To quiet the poor without delay.
He bade them to his great barn repair,
And they should have food for the winter there.

Rejoiced at such tidings good to hear,
The poor folk flock'd from far and near;
The great barn was full as it could hold
Of women and children, young and old.

Then when he saw it could hold no more,
Bishop Hatto he made fast the door;
And while for mercy on Christ they call,
Set fire to the barn, and burnt them all.

„I 'faith 'tis an excellent bonfire!" quoth he,
„And the country is greatly obliged to me,
For ridding it, in these times forlorn,
Of rats that only consumse the corn.

So then to his palace returned he
And he sat down to supper merrily,
And he slept that night like an innocent man,
But Bishop Hatto ne'er slept again.

In the morning as he enter'd the hall
Where his picture hung against the wall
A sweat like death all o'er him came.
For the rats had eaten it out of the frame.

As he look'd there came a man from his farm,
He had a countenance white with alarm.
„Mylord, I open'd your granaries this morn,
And the rats had eaten all your corn."

Another came running presently,
And he was pale as pale could be;
„Fly! my lord bishop, fly,“ quoth he,
„Ten thousand rats are coming this way,
The Lord forgive you for yesterday!“

„I'll go to my tow'r on the Rhine“, replied he
„'Tis the safest place in Germany;
The walls are high and the shores are steep,
And the stream is strong and the water deep.“

Bishop Hatto fearfully hasten'd away,
And he crossed the Rhine without delay
And reach'd his tower, and barr'd with care
All the windows, door and loop holes there.

He laid him down, and closed his eyes; —
But soon a scream made him arise,
He started, and saw two eyes of flame
On his pil'ow, from whence the screaming came.

He listen'd and look'd; it was only the cat;
But the bishop he grew more fearful for that,
For she sat screaming, mad with fear
At the army of rats, that were drawing near.

For they have swam o'er the river so deep,
And they have climb'd the shores so steep.
And now by thousands up they crawl
To the holes and windows in the wall.

Down on his knees the bishop fell,
And faster and faster his beads did tell,
As louder and louder, drawing near,
The saw of their teeth without he could hear.

12

And in at the windows, and in at the door
And through the walls by thousands they pour,
And down through the ceiling and up through the floor,
From the right and the left, from behind and before
From within and without, from above and below.

And all at once to the bishop they go,
They have whetted their teeth against the stones,
And now they pick the bishop's bones;
They gnaw'd the flesh from every limb,
For they were sent to judgment on him. —

Southey.

*   *   *

Another event shows us the Mouse-tower not in connexion with atrocious crimes, but as the scene of noble deeds and patriotic enthusiasm.

In the thirty years-war the Swedes took possession of all the fortresses and castles along the Rhine. Ehrenfels had been taken and now the Swedes laid siege to Hatto's tower, to become by its conquest masters of the passage of the Rhine. But it was no easy task, to gain it, for it was defended by the knights of the Teutonic order, who, in spite of the enemy's superiority, accepted the combat.

They fought bravely, but overpowered by the enemy they all found a glorious death.

A single knight still resisted in spite of his numerous wounds. His heroic valour excited the admiration of the enemy and their commander summoned him to surrender.

„Neither mercy for you, nor for me: knights can die, but not surrender.

Saying this the valiant knight seized the astonished enemies and plunged into the river. Vainly the Swedes sought for his corpse and especially for the flag, but the Rhine had buried them both.

Rüdesheim.

night Broemser, inspired by the sermons of St. Bernhard, who preached at Spire, took the cross, like others, who were present and departed for Palestine, leaving his little daughter as an orphan at Rüdesheim.

Knight Broemser was a brave warrior, who had seen many bloody victories and before whose sword the Saracens fled with terror. Valiant in war, but jovial over the cup, firm in his resolutions, neither prayers, nor entreaties could detain him from the execution of them.

As a proof of his heroic valour, it is told, that, when he was in distant countries, he killed a dragon, which did much harm to the crusaders, and many other glorious deeds are reported of him, which we need not repeat, as the dragon's death is a sufficient proof of his strenght and courage.

One day the knight was surprised by the

Saracens, who surrounded him and without hope
of deliverance or succour from his countrymen
he resolved, to yield his life, only at a high price.
He opened a passage for himself through the
surrounding infidels, who fell like corn under
the sithe of the reaper. Fatigued and exhausted
by his wounds, he sunk down and was bound,
hand and foot placed on a swift horse and hur-
riedly placed in safety.

He wore for many years the chains of slav-
ery and was obliged to perform the meanest
tasks; at length he made a vow to consecrate
his daughter to God, and happening to break
his chains, he killed his overseer and fled. His
comrades received him joyfully, but the knight
thought of his promise, and prepared to return
to his country.

He was received with joy and affection at
Rüdesheim, especially by his beautiful and
blooming daughter; but she was struck with
dismay and terror, when her father informed
her of his vow and of his firm resolution, to
accomplish it.

In vain the girl implored for mercy declaring
that she had been betrothed during his absence.
The knight was inexorable and threatened her
with his malediction. Driven almost to madness
by the thought that her father had cursed her,

she became desperate and hidden by the shadows of night, trew herself into the Rhine.

Some fishermen found her corpse the next morning and carried it to the castle; the knight was in the greatest despair at this sight and accused himself of his daughter's murder.

When his grief subsided he promised as an atonement for his crime, to build a church. But by the dissipations, in which he plunged to stifle his grief and pain, he forgot his promise, until his daughter appeared to him, one night looking at him with a countenance full of tender and melancholy sweetness; the chains, which he had born in the East, fell at this moment with a crash on the floor and roused him from his sleep.

The sun began to colour the sky, when discontented with himself and with a throbbing heart he paced the battlements of his castle, to cool his excitement in the fresh morning-breeze.

Suddenly he heard loud cries; some peasants approached him with an image of the holy Virgin; they said, that when they wer ploughing, the oxen had drawn it from the earth and the image called for help.

This seemed to the knight an admonition from heaven and he immediately ordered a chapel to be built and the image to be put in it. Beside the chapel some years later was built the convent, named: „Noth Gottes." (Gods help.)

The dragon's teeth and the chains which the knight bore are still preserved in the castle of Johannisberg, property of the prince of Metternich, which he got in 1816 as a fee from the Emperor Francis of Austria.

Ehrenfels.

Uta sat at the window of her chamber looking towards Reichenstein, which was surrounded by huge, dark rocks, the outlines of which were sketched on the darkblue sky. — She sat with folded hands and wept bitterly, because her father had insulted Reichenstein, whom she loved, and called him a robber, whom the emperor had out-lawed.

She retired to her room excusing herself to her father under the plea of indisposition. She entered her chamber with tottering steps, sat down at a window and watched the waves of the Rhine, illuminated by the silver-rays of the moon. Suddenly she trembled with anguish and terror and could scarcely breathe, as she saw a mass of flames and smoke rise to the sky just above the castle of Reichenstein and soon flames broke from the windows and dark figures could be seen as if fighting desperately.

„Holy Virgin, protect him!" exclaimed she „It is impossible! My eyes deceive me! He a robber and his castle in flames!

She shaded her eyes with both hands, and looked again; Reichenstein was burning and the emperors sentence was executed.

Pale and tearless Uta recognised in the destruction of Reichenstein the wreck of her happines; she saw a small boat cross the river and approach Ehrenfels. „Uta! Uta!" sounded a voice through the stillness of the night, „Oh come, that I may see you once more and for the last time!"

It was the voice of her lover, who implored her to come to him; overpowered by her feeling she hastened down stairs and drew herself in his arms.

„I am an outlaw and fugitive, Uta. My castle is destroyed and I was scarcely able to save my life and some jewels, to prevent me from starving in distant lands. Farewell, I leave you for ever and even if the world curses me, you will shed some tears of pity and love for me!"

„Oh, my beloved!" said she sobbing and pressing him tenderly to her bosom. „It would have been better, that we had died in our happy days, than to be obliged, to separate now, under such circumstances!"

„Uta, I can't live without you; fly with me;

I can't leave you, charming maid. I love you too much!

„I cannot abandon my father. I will take the veil as soon as you are gone and devote to you all my thoughts."

„No never!" cried he, then throwing his arm around her and stepping some paces back, he plunged into the Rhine.

Not a cry was heard; only the waves caused by the splash and then the river flowed tranquilly on.

The next day the lovers' corpses were found in close embrace.

Rheinstein.

hose, who have made the tour of the Rhine, will doubtless know this stately castle, which was restored by the king of Prussia and rebuilt in the style of the middle age.

Below Rheinstein near Trechtlingshausen is situated the old fortress of Reichenstein and above Rheinstein, on the right shore, is to be seen Ehrenfels. Between Rheinstein and Reichenstein are to be found the ruins of the church of St. Clemens, owergrown with weeds and ivy and seeming to mourn for its passed grandeur.

There lived once in the castle of Rheinstein a charming girl under the severe guardianship of her father; who since his wife's death led a contemplative, melancholy life. His charming little daughter could alone bring a smile on his face, for she was the only being, whom he loved.

Knight Seyfried was nothwithstanding his love of solitude not of a truly affectionate character. He had many frailties and especially that of thinking the happiness of his daughter could be founded on external splendour and show. The maid loved the knight of Reichenstein, a brave, fine fellow, but poor and possessing nothing besides his castle, his sword and merry humour. The knight Kurt of Ehrenfels, a malicious deceitful old bachelor, was his nearest relation. Kuno opened his heart to him and begged him to speak to the father and in his name ask for the daughter's hand, declaring that he could not live without her.

„Hm!" said Kurt, „it is madness, Cuno, to think of matrimony. Do like me and you will be much more comfortable!"

„It is imposible", replied Cuno, „the girl has wound herself around my heart and sooner would I renounce all hopes of heaven, than leave her."

„Well!" murmured Kurt, „if it must be so, I will content myself. Women are caught most easily by presents; so I hope, you have something for her, that will render my words more impressive."

„Cousin, do you wish to drive me mad? Do you think, that Gerda is as mean and pitiless, as the women of your acquaintance? But now I remember something, which you may offer her as my present. In my stable I have a beautiful horse, which I myself received as a gift, but that makes no difference. It is better with her, than with me!"

Charmed by this thought he ordered the horse to be led forth and accompanied the clumsy Kurt to the foot of castle Rheinstein.

Scarce had Kurt seen the lovely girl than his heart was inflamed by passionate love and he resolved instead of wooing for Cuno, to have her for himself. He spoke to Seyfried, informed him his cousin's wish and bade him take his choise between booth.

The weak old knight, allured by Kurt's fortune gave him not only the preference, but he resolved, to baffle every attempt of Cuno, even by force of arms. The sly, hipocritical Kurt told Cuno, that Gerda loved him sincerely and that she had entreated her father, to grant their union, but the old knight had rebuffed the marriage-proposal and therefore every attempt of getting his consent was in vain.

The young man hearing this news strode in despair through his castle. He thought of the most adventurous plans for the possession of his beloved and he could not find a moment of rest; after having several times tried in vain to speak to the father and having been driven from Rheinstein, a deep discouragement seized him and he abandoned all hope. Now Kurt thought the time favourable, to gain favour with the young girl; he paid her great attentions, but she, frightened and disgusted, shunned him, for she had put all her confidence in Cuno. She revealed to her father her love for Cuuo and implored him to give his consent. Seyfried would hear nothing about it and at once fixed the day of her marriage with Kurt.

The night following this determination was for Gerda one of the most painful and afflicting. She wept and lamented all the night long, till she at last, weary and exhausted fell asleep. She dreamed that Cuno approached her bed and imprinted a fervent kiss on her lips, saying:

„Why, will you not fly and take refuge with me?“

Gerda awoke doubting, whether it was illusion or reality. At this moment she heard a soft neighing from the stable, which she took as a good omen.

„Yes,“ exclaimed she resolutely, „I will prepare for the wedding and his horse instead of carrying me into the castle of him I hate, shall bear me to the arms of my beloved Cuno!“

Kurt heard with rapture that the lord of Rheinstein had granted his suit; he mocked the wrath of his cousin and gave the necessary orders for a splendid and brilliant weddiug.

The day at last arrived and Gerda chosed the church of St. Clemens for the ceremony of exchanging the rings; the procession was obliged to return to Rheinstein and from there to move towards Ehrenfels. But Gerda had before prudently given notice of her plan to her lover, who waited with throbbing heart for the day, which should render him for ever happy.

The bells were ringing solemnly! the long and brilliant procession moved towards the chapel. The lovely bride was richly adorned with pearls and precious stones; she discerned lighted candles on the altar, when on a sudden Gerda spurred the horse, which her lover had sent her as a present and galloped toward Reichenstein.

Kurt was the first, who recovered from his surprise. He pursued her with curses and imprecations, followed by the father and some knights curious to see the issue of this strange affair.

Cuno, who was on the look-out, seeing with an inexpressible joy the bride approaching his castle in full speed, oppened the gate and having helped her in alighting from the horse, embraced her tenderly and imprinted passionate kisses on her lips, then barred the gate closely. Soon after when the father came and demanded entrance. the happy young bridegroom refused it and threatened to pursue them with arms, if they dared to trouble him further. The procession, which followed slowly, found the corpse of Kurt on the way who had fallen from his horse. Cuno was his lawful heir and the wedding, instead of at Ehrenfels, was celebrated in the castle of Reichenstein, to the great satisfaction of all and even old Seyfried.

———

St. Clemens church.

n the former tradition the church of St. Clemens was mentioned, the foundation of which may not be without interest.

A noble young lady in „Sauerthal" had, at the death of her parents, become heiress of a considerable fortune, which together with her fascinating beauty allured a great many admirers and wooers.

At this time there lived in the castle of Rheinstein a brave and resolute fellow, whose valour was surpassed only by his excessive impudence, with which he derided the laws. He saw one day the lovely Ina and her beauty as well as her fortune made him resolve to win her. He was not the man for flirting and uttering tender sighs. But firmly resolved, to attain his end, he sent a messenger to her with a marriage-proposal. After having received her refusal he assembled his men and marched with them to the „Sauerthal", to obtain by force, what the young lady would not grant willingly.

It was a dark and gloomy night, the sky was covered with clouds and the wind moaned through the mountains, while in the valley reigned a deep silence, as if with fear and anxious expectation of the coming storm. Silently the armed party left the Rheinstein and wound their way through the forest, so as to attain their aim more surely. The horse's hoofs sounded hollowly on the damp ground and not a sound was heard but the noise of the rider's armour.

At lenght they arrived at the lady's castle; the knight made a sign, at which the most part of his troop stopped and alighted; they gently approached the gate and two messengers were despatched, with the order to demand admission and immediately to kill the man, who opened the gate.

The wanderers were willingly admitted. But no sooner had the keeper opened, than he fell pierced through with a sword. The war-note of the knight was blown and his troop entered the castle without resistance.

The war-cry re-echoed wildly through the deserted corridors and roused the surprised soldiers from their sleep. The commander sprang to arms and led his men against the intruders. But he was at last obliged to retire, overpowered

by the number. In the mean while the knight
had carried the fainting girl out of the castle
and putting her on his horse fled at full gallop,
protected by his soldiers.

They rode on towards the bank of the Rhine
where a large boat awaited them, which they
entered triumphantly. The boatmen seized the
oars and began rowing to the opposite shore.

But a thunder-storm seemed to have reserved
its violence for this moment. The wind howled
through the oaks and firs of the mountains, threw
itself furiously on the boat and pushed it out
on the foaming waves. The most courageous
were struck with fear and grew pale with terror;
they tried to gain the land by rowing with every
exertion. But their efforts were in vain; the
boat, hurled along by the wind, swiftly approached the rocks in the middle of the stream.

In this desperate moment the maid, who had
till now been stupiefied, recovered her senses and
understood with terror her dangerous situation;
she knelt down to pray and vowed to build a
chapel to the honour of St. Clemens, if he would
deliver her from the robber's hand and rescue
her from the present danger.

As soon as she had finished this prayer, a
violent shock threw her on the ground and at
the same time a crash was heard, mingled with
the cries of despair. Ina closed her eyes, that

13*

she might not see the waves, which rose foaming and roaring about her, but with surprise she saw, that, instead of sinking, she was lifted up miraculously and carried through the air.

When Ina had god used to the splendour, which dazzled her eyes, she perceived herself in the Saint's arms, who looked tenderly at her and laid her softly down on the shore.

The tunder-storm had ceased and the moon re-appeared through the dark clouds.

Arrived at the shore and seeing herself in security, the maid fell upon her knees, to return thanks to the Saint, but he had dissappeared. It was the break of day, when her servants, who had soon after her disappearance left the castle to pursue the robbers, found their lady unhurt and safe in a fisherman's cottage.

The knight with his men had perished in the Rhine and their corpses were found the next day on the shore.

Ina, faithful to her vow, built the church of St. Clemens and when it was finished, she appeared before the altar as the bride of a valiant and noble young knight.

The church, as we have before mentioned, is now a ruin.

Falkenburg.

iba, the lovely daugther of the castellan of the imperial fortress of Falkenburg, lived there in peacable and modest retirement with her mother.

The father had died a long while ago and had left to his daughter, besides an education adapted to those times, a considerable fortune, which was still increased by the prudent economy and saving of her mother.

A great number of admirers, allured by the loveliness and virtues of this charming and modest maid, sought her hand. But Liba refused them all, for her heart was already engaged, she loved a young knight of the neighbourhood, who promised to marry her as soon, as the „pfalsgrave“ had invested him with his fief.

One fine May-day, when the fields and the meadows were adorned with fresh verdure, the vines promised a rich vintage and the buds and flowers bloomed so sweetly, while the birds chirped and a pair of turtle-doves, the favourites of Liba, were billing and cooing. Liba sat at her window, to inhale the fresh fragrant air of spring and looked from the balcony at the river, on which dark ships sailed carrying the pro-ductions of distant countries to flourishing towns. „Mother“, exclaimed Liba, „how happy I would be, if Guntram returned to day!“

Scarce had she uttered these words, when she suddenly rose from her seat, with a loud cry of joy; she descended into the court-yard and hastened towards the gate.

· The mother looked inquiringly after her daugh-ter and went instantly to the window, where Liba had been sitting.

The young girl was already some hundred paces distant from the castle, offering her beau-tiful rosy lips to a young knight, who had just alighted from his horse.

The happy pair walked arm in arm or rather ran up the hill on which the castle stood and saluted the mother tenderly, who seemed to grow young again, at seeing the happiness of her child.

After Guntram had admired the beauty of the small garden cultivated by Liba, he sat down at her side, to give an account of all, that had occured and informed her, that he was on the way to the „pfalsgrave“, to obtain his grant· He looked tenderly at his beloved and she softly

pressed his hand, when he spoke of his hopes
and of the joy of soon having a home and fire-
side of his own.

„Farewell now", he said „the time presses;
I shall soon return and then remain for ever
with you: and you, Liba", continued he smiling,
„prepare your nuptial dress, for I will wait no
longer; I am burning with desire to see you in
my castle, which seems to me so sad and gloomy
without you. Don't detain me; cried he, when
she begged him to stay longer „what has to be
done, had better be done soon!" He pressed
his betrothed once more to his bosom, kissed the
tears from her eyes and descended into the
court-yard, where the horse, waiting impatiently
for its rider, neighed joyously at the sight of him.

Guntram was a noble young man. His figure
was pleasing and manly; his conversation and
manners gained the pfalsgrave's favour and as
the latter wanted an ambassador for Burgundy,
he chose Guntram for this honourable office.
The young man was obliged to accept it, but
with regret. He sent a messenger to Liba, to
announce to her his appointment and begged her
to excuse his absence.

Liba received the messenger with aching
heart and reproached herself, for not being able
to quiet the inexpressible fear she felt; she imagined a dark cloud had covered the sun of her

happiness and she saw in the future a misfortune, of which she could not give an exact account to herself.

Since the last leave-taking of Guntram, she was not as sprightly, as before; her temper seemed thoroughly changed. The sun seemed to her not to shine so brightly, the flowers not to bloom as beautifully and the birds sing as merrily, as in former times. Her garden had no charms for her now and she sat all day long at the window, surveying the road, by which he must return.

In the mean while Guntram's embassy was at end. With a joyful heart he travelled homewards, and hastening, impatient to see his Liba again, with winged steps left his companions far behind.

One day he took a side-road, leading to a forest, in which he lost his way. He hoped, to meet somebody, who could bring him back to the right road, but it was in vain. He at last arrived before a solitary, half decayed castle.

The knight entered the court-yard joyously and gave his horse to a boy, who was quite surprised at seeing him and stared at him, as if he was an apparition from another world. „Where is your master?“ asked Guntram. The boy showed him a gray tower, overgrown with ivy, into which the knight entered. The young man felt a strange excitement, when he mounted the stone staircase his steps sounding hollowly through the old place.

It seemed to him, as if he were in an enchanted castle and all fairy-tales, which he had heard or read, rose up in his mind.

He was received by an old man, who told him, that he was the keeper and led the stranger into a gloomy apartment, where he bade him wait, till he had announced him.

Surprised at such an odd and at the same time solemn reception, he entered and saw opposite him a veiled picture, which excited his wonder and curiosity as well, as the oldfashioned furniture of the room. Moved by an irresistible desire of discovering the mystery, which seemed to hover over the castle, he lifted up the veil and instantly started back with surprise; for he saw the portrait of a wonderfully beautiful lady, who looked smilingly at him.

At the same time he thought he heard the soft and melancholy tunes of a harp sound through the room. The young man had not yet recovered from his surprise, when the keeper returned introducing a thin old man, who received him as the lord of the castle saying:

„We are seldom visited by a stranger, but nevertheless you may be assured, that, though we live here retired, we shall not forget the customs of hospitality. Therefore you are welcome!"

The old man spoke in a proud, but grave manner. Guntram felt a strange fear, but which was soon dissipated by the old man's politeness, so that he replied with affability and confidence.

He became by degrees accustomed to the gloom, which surounded him and after having emptied some glasses of an excellent wine with the lord of the castle, his tongue was free'd and he conversed about every thing regarding chivalry, tournaments, warfares and minstrelsy.

„You also seem to be very fond of music, for I see there a harp, which seems to mourn on account of its inactivity."

In saying the last words he fixed his eyes upon the lord of the castle, for he thought by alluding to the harp he could know something of the vailed portrait. But he stopped short, when he perceived the face of the old man become gloomy and sighing covered his eyes with his hands.

„You are right, Sir!" replied he sadly, „once its tones were clear and melodius; but now its strings are broken, like the happiness of my life. Good night and sleep well, if you can."

Having said this, he rose and withdrew, accompanied by the keeper, to his apartment.

The young man remained confused, for he saw with regret, that he had re-opened the wound, which gave to this gloomy abode such a melancholy character.

When the keeper returned, he found him sitting at the table and leaning his head upon his hands.

„Knight“, said he, „my lord prays you, to remain one day longer with him and he excuses himself to have left you so suddenly. But you have touched a cord, which always re-opens the wound, which has rendered him old and unsociable“.

„A strange mystery reigns in this castle“; continued Guntram „could you not explain it to me?“

„Why not, knight? Come with me to your room and on the way I will give you the wished for explanation“.

Guntram rose and followed the keeper into the adjoining room, where the vailed portrait hung.

„Stop here“, said he, „before all and tell me, why this charming portrait is covered with this ugly veil?“

„Have you already seen her?“ asked the old man. „It is the daughter of the house, painted when she still lived in glory with us. You see how beautiful she was; but unfortunately she

was a „coquette" and capricious, but nevertheless she was amiable, for she was of a fascinating, bewitching beauty".

The old man was silent some moments, like
one sunk in deep melancholy revery; then he
continued:

„A great deal of admirers wooed her, amongst
them a young man, the last descendant of an
illustrious family and at the same time the support of his old, infirm mother, to whom he devoted all his cares. This maid was, as I have
said of a wild capricious and extravacant gaiety.
She demanded of her lovers things inpracticable
and drove them away in this manner. Only the
young man, whom we have mentioned, remained
faithful to her, for his love was a sincere one
and he had already done a great many things
which were almost impossible for her sake. As
a last task she imposed on him, to descent into
the ancestoral vault and to bring her a crown
of gold which must be found on the head of one
of her ancestors; the lover did as he was bidden
and profaned the tombs.

This profanation was punished. On the next
morning they found the young man's corpse in
the vault, holding the stolen crown in his hand.
A stone loosened from the vault's roof had
killed him.

When the mother heard this horrible news,

she died some days after. In her last moments she cursed the extravagant folly of the maid, who had caused her son's death. From thence the maid pined away and died in the following year on the same day, as her lover. But when they wanted to bury her, the coffin was empty and the corpse had disappeared."

At the end of the tale they arrived at the bed-room. The keeper put the wax-light on the table and wished him good night, but he returned again to the door and said:

„Knight, if during the night some strange thing should happen, say but a „pater noster" and continue to sleep."

He withdrew and the noise of his steps resounding through the corridors increased the trouble of the young man.

The wine which he had drunk and the last admonition of the keeper had put him in a strange excitement. What were the meaning of his words? What sort of spectre haunted the castle?" such were the questions, which troubled his mind and filled him with fear. Drowsiness oppressed his eyelids and dressed as he was he threw himself on the bed to enjoy a few moments of rest.

He could but slumber; suddenly it seemed to him as if he heard a light noise, like the rustling of a lady's gown, from the adjoining room;

he listened again, but all was silent and he discontent with himself replaced his head on the pillow. In this moment he heard the soft tunes of a harp; clever hands touched its strings, sounding harmoniously and accompanied by a sweet, melancholy voice. Seized by a mingled feeling of fear and rapture he rose and approached the door softly, through a crevice of which he perceived the original of the portrait in a light night dress, the harp of gold leaning on her knees: her charming face had the expression of a deep melancholy and when she had finished, she let the harp fall on the ground with a cry of acute pain and distress.

Guntram could not contain his curiosity any longer. He opened the door and stepped in. The maid looked at him not with fear and anger, but with a melancholy regard of love, which penetrated deep into the joung man's heart. Being no longer master of himself, he sunk at her feet and kissed the hand, which she offered him; she drew him softly near to her and pressed him passionately to her bosom, abandoning her lips to his kisses with a sweet rapture.

„You love me!" said she sighing.

„Oh more than my life!" replied he trembling.

The maid took a ring and put it on his finger; e phressed her to his breast, but in the same

moment he heard the death-cry of a screech-owl
and he held in his arms a corpse.

Astonished and frightened he returned with
tottering steps to his room, where nearly deprived
of sense he sank on his couch. When on the
next morning the suns rays penetrated through
the windows, he awoke, rubbed his eyes and
collected his thoughts. He thought, it must have
been an illusion, but when he perceived the ring
on his finger, he was convinced, that it was no
dream, but a reality. He wanted to pull it off
and throw it away, but he could not. The ring
seemed to have grown on his finger. Pale and
restless he walked to and fro in his room. His
mind was troubled with feverish excitement by
the remembrance of that what had happened and
by his infidelity to Liba. He resolved at once
to depart and to fly from a place, where an extravagant love had seduced him, to commit an
act, which would always torment him.

The lord of the castle entered, to inquire
after his health. „You seem to have spent a bad
night, Sir; you look pale and sad, or . . . ."

„What room is this, where we are?" interrupted the young man quickly.

„The only one, which is habitable! it was
my daughter's apartment!"

„Yes, yes," exclaimed Guntram sighing, „there
is her toilet and I have seen her this night."

„Sir", cried the keeper, perceiving the ring,
„who has given you this ring?"

„She herself!"

„Then God help you! In three times nine
days you will be a corpse!"

Guntram started like one condemned; he
wanted to speak, but his tongue moved not; he
wanted to laugh, but his features became distorted
and regarding himself at that moment in the
looking glass he fell with a loud cry on the
floor.

Guntram, though in a paroxysm of fever, set
out on his way home some hours after. His heart
was oppressed and his eyes glowed like fire. A
crowd of ravens flying and croaking over him
made him shudder, while his horse, as if perceiving his master's situation, ran in full gallop
homewards.

The joy of his betrothed was unutterable,
when she could, after so long an absence, press
the beloved youth to her heart; she perceived
at once, that he was gloomy and dejected and
that a secret oppressed him, but she understood
too at once, the mind of a man may be troubled
by other dissappointments than that of a woman.

Guntram, taking comfort from the presence
of the lovely maid and perceiving a diminution
of his passion, pressed impatiently upon the
celebration of the wedding and Liba could only

reply by kisses, for she longed as passionately as he to see this happy day.

The day arrived at last. Guntram approached the altar with the sweet hope, that the charm, which chained him, would be broken by the nuptial benediction and he felt for the first time more tranquil and happy.

He approached the altar with the firm persuasion, that he was about to perform an act as important, as it was salutary for him. But when the priest joined their hands, he grew pale, tottered and fell to the ground with a frightful scream.

He was carried home; Liba, seized with despair, fell upon his neck, with a flood of tears and uttering his name.

At lenght he recovered his senses, he looked with astonishment around him; he then remembered what had happened; tears filled his eyes and he leant his head upon his love's bosom. When he had entirely recovered, he related to her the adventure of Walburg; he told her, that he had been overpowered by a wild delusion and that the dead girl had appeared and put her hand into his at the altar.

„Liba", said he sighing, „I atone for my fault by death; forgive me and become my wife, before I die; for I feel, that I will find no rest and I shall be unhappy for ever!"

14

Liba kissed his burning lips fervently and sent for a priest, whom she led to the bed of the dying man; the nuptial benediction was uttered and Guntram, after having once more pressed his wife to his bosom, uttered a deep sigh, lifted up his eyes to heaven and expired.

The inconsolable wife did not shed one tear: her grief was too deep and afficting, she entered a convent and some years after died calmly. She was interred at the side of her lover.

Her mother did not outlive her long.

Heimburg.

eyond Niederheimbach rise the ruins of Heimburg, in the neighbourhood of which, on a rock, stands the castle of Sonneck, which majestically overlooks the valley of Fluthen (Fluthenthal).

Heimburg was built in the early ages, by Sueno who is renowned as one of the bravest warriors who fought under the command of king Pharamond against Rome and the Gauls. Worms is supposed to have been built by Pharamond and had in the beginning the name of Pharamundia, then Pharmatia, Vormatia and lastly Worms.

Frankenthal is supposed to have existed at the same time.

But to resume our story, Sueno was appointed commander of the troops, which occupied the newly conquered part of Nothern Gaul, while Pharamoud departed, to meet the enemy, coming from the South.

One day he received a message, that his daughter, to whom since her mother's death he had devoted all his tenderness!, had given birth to a boy.

Angry and in despair by the disgrace to his family he hastened home and when the trembling girl refused to name her seducer, he with one blow of his fist felled her to the ground, and killed her.

Sueno remained in solitary retirement in his castle, for grief and repentance made him gloomy and morose. Pharamond visited him one day, to ask for the hand of his daughter. The father led him silently to her tomb, and when he had explained to him the cause of the maid's death, the king, provoked by grief and rage, drew his sword and stabbed him to the heart.

He tock the boy with him, for it was his child and he was the seducer.

———

Lorch.

n the neighbourhood of the town of Lorch is to be seen a steep rock, called the „Kedderich". It was inhabited by mountain-sprites and a great many things are related of them.

One of the prettiest tradition is that of the devil's ladder, which I shall now relate.

Sibo of Lorch after his wife's death became a morose and sulky old fellow, who could only be cheered by the sight of his daughter, who was very lovely. He was a misanthrope and shut himself in his castle and refused hospitality to all travellers; everybody tried to avoid him and his castle.

One evening a knock was heard at the castle gate. The knight, who happened to be in his worst humor, embraced this opportunity to give vent to his anger and sent the strangers who claimed hospitality away, uttering the most abusive words against them.

When he asked after his daughter the following day, he was told, that she had gone to the fields and had not been seen since.

He immediately dispatched messengers for her, but they returned at noon without having found her; they had only heard from a shepherd, that he had seen two little gray men, who took the maid in their arms and climbed up the steep declivity of the „Kederich" with her.

Great was the knights consternation at this news. He ran immediately towards the rock, called his daughter's name and saw her accompanied by a little gray man, who made him a sign crying:

„This is the reward for your refusal to us yesterday; when you know, how to show hospitality, better, I shall give her back to you, Sir knight!"

Then he departed with a loud laughter, taking the maid with him and left the father to despair.

Years passed away and the knight went every day, so see his daughter, who walked in the morning and evening on the rock. She advanced in years and the ardent desire of seeing her father again, rendered her life on the mountain disagreable and gloomy.

Now it happened, that a friend of her childhood returned home and repaired instantly to

Sibo's castle; he heard with dismay what had happened and went speedily to the „Kederich", to deliver the maid.

The maid walked up and down the rock, her rosy face illuminated by the golden rays of the setting sun and appeared in her snow-white gown like an angel from above. All the fire of love which the young man had felt for her from his childhood and which had still increased, burnt fiercer at her sight; he called her by name and climbed the rocks, till he sunk down exhausted, and covering his face with both hands. He remained a long time in this position, the last rays of the setting sun had disappeared from the horizon, on which the stars and moon shone with a soft light, and he still sat at the foot of the mountain, meditating upon the means of delivering his beloved; but in vain, for it was impossible to climp the „Kedderich".

„Ah!" exclaimed he with a deep sigh. „Who can help me?"

„Why are you so dejected?" stammered a woman appearing suddenly before him. „If you wish to deliver the maid, return to-morrow evening, for it is high time, to marry her and the father is punished severely enough."

The young man, recovering from his surprise, asked who she was and if she were indeed able to help him.

„She has been my child since she was carried hither and I took care of her with a mother's love. She spoke often of you and seeing your grief, I will help you, if you are still inclined to marry her. She longs to see you again!"

The youth swore, that he loved her and would never love another; the little woman listened to him and nodding her head praised his sentiments.

„Return to morrow evening and climb the rock; I shall have made the way practicable by then."

Having said this, she disappeared as suddenly as she had come and the young man returned with a joyous and grateful heart to the father, whom he informed of his adventure, expressing the hope of bringing the maid home the next day.

On the following evening Sibo went with the young knight and found, a ladder leaning against the „Kedderich" reaching from the foot to the top of the rock. The youth mounted the steps courageosly, while the old man watched the lover with a palpitating heart, till he had reached the last step. Arrived at the summit of the rock he waved his hat triumphantly, and with loud cries of joy he entered the large caves before him, to search for the maid.

He had scarce advanced a few paces, when

he suddenly found himself in an enchanted region. Superb flowers, which he had never seen before, exhaled the sweetest fragrance; rivulets as clear as cristal ran with a soft noise over stones of various colours and the most melodius sounds were heard from the surrounding grove. He was led on by a magical power and arrived at a blooming grove from the depht of which a rosy light issued and brightened his way. He advanced and came at last to a grotto, the walls of which shone brightly from the reflection of the light, which had attracted him. In the grotto he found the maid, slumbering on a bank of moss and in her dream extending her arms towards him.

The youth knelt down before her and kissed the border of her gown. She awoke by the stranger's touch, was frightened and wanted to escape, but he detained her making himself known to her and promising to lead her home to her father. She now recognised her friend and suffered him to embrace and kiss her. A hollow noise disturbed them. A dwarf stood before them, whose gloomy and threatening eyes forebode mischief, but the little woman, who had bid the youth to come, joined them and spoke to the dwarf in a strange language, both began to laugh and the goblin said:

„Well, young man, the bride is yours, for it

is in vain we fight against the artifices of women; take her away and never violate the laws of chivalry and hospitality, for if you do you will become much unhappier, than the old Sibo!

Grateful and happy the young man was about to take away his beloved with him; but the dwarf opposed, saying:

„No, my friend, return the way, by which you came hither; we will lead your bride a safer way. He took the maid's hand and led her away. The young man returned speedily by the way, which he had come.

Below he found the maid in the arms of her father and when the sprites took leave of them, they delivered to the maid a small box, saying:

„There is your dowry, child, and when you celebrate your wedding, whe shall return and pay you a visit.“

And so they did. The wedding was celebrated merrily and after the guests had retired and the young pair were still together and conversing about their future life, they saw the two sprites entering, who brought them nuptial presents and rejoiced to see their foster-child a happy wife.

Peace and happiness reigned now in the castle and in course of time lovely grand-children played around old Sibo, whose melancholy had, since the severe lesson given to him, entirely dissappeared.

The ladder stood in the same place for a long time, but it fell to pieces through age. The people living in the neighbourhood had called it the „devil's-ladder", a name, which the walls carry till the present day.

———————

Pfalzgrafenstein.

elow Bacharach, opposite Caub, on a rock in the middle of the Rhine is to be seen a gloomy castle, called „Pfalsgrafenstein".

The „Pfalzgraf" Conrad of Staufen, a brother-in-law of the emperor Frederick the first, who inherited the estates after the death of Hermann of Stahleck, had a beautiful daughter, but no sons. Illustrious princes contended, to obtain the hand of the rich heiress, but in vain: she had already devoted her heart to a young man, who besides possessing a chivalrous disposition also heroic courage and prudence: it was Henry the lion, chief of the „Welfs".

Henry having heard of the matchless beauty of Agnes, resolved to repair to the Rhine, to see her. Disguised as a pilgrim he entered the castle during the counts absence. He was introduced to the ladies apartment, to shorten the tediousness of the evening for them by singing and relating his adventures.

Pfalzgrafenstein

Mainz Halenza's Verlag

He stood with surprise and admiration before the lovely girl.

Agnes was likewise not indifferent. Her cheeks glowed, her bosom heaved and she felt her heart beat quicker and a strange excitement overcome her.

The mother perceived at once the danger of the pilgrim's presence. She dismissed him with few words, resolving however to make inquiry about his true rank, for she had already seen, he was no common pilgrim. But all this was unnecessary. The pilgrim was once more announced and having been admitted he made himself known to her and begged the mother, to use her influence with the „Pfalzgraf" and persuade him, not to reject his marriage-proposal on account of political reasons.

The delighted mother, who had already at the first meeting felt a lively sympathy for the stranger and was now the more prepossessed in his favor, instantly sent for her daughter, represented her the knight in his true character and then withdrew, for she wished eagerly to see both united as soon as possible

Her wish was fulfilled. Agnes confessed her love; swore fidelity to the enthusiastic young man and sunk on the bosom of her mother, who approached to bless their union. On the next day Henry departed in his disguise and he would return later as duke, openly to demand the hand of his beloved.

As the mother was interested in marrying her daughter to Henry, so the „Pfalzgraf" and the emperor were interested in marrying her to a prince of their family.

Scarce had Conrad of Staufen heard, that the chief of the „Welfs" wooed his daughter with greater success than the others, and that his wife took his part, he gave orders, to furnish the castle on the Rhine, which he had recently built and to imprison his daughter there.

The mother however, offended by this act, thought upon a stratagem and dispatched a messenger to Henry, to inform him of what had happened; she told him to come and celebrate his marriage with Agnes in secret.

Henry followed the invitation with joyful haste. A young priest was bribed and in 'a disguise led by the „Pfalzgräfin" into the castle. The duke swam to the castle and received dry clothes from the bribed sentinel, who opened the gate.

The nuptial benediction was performed and the young couple left to themselves.

The mother joyfully withdrew, to communicate to her husband what had happened. She did it with so much grace and loveliness, that the „Pfalzgraf's" anger was appeased.

But to have revenge for the trick, which she

played him, he gave orders, that Agnes and her husband should remain imprisoned in the castle, till the young woman had given birth to a boy. He then speedily repaired to the emperor, to give him an account of what had happened. The emperor was obliged to conceal his anger and give his approval. It is unnecessary, to tell, that Agnes and her husband readily consented to the conditions imposed upon them.

In remembrance of this blissful captivity in the tower a law was made, by which each „Pfalzgräfin" was bound to remain in the castle till the birth of a child.

Gutenfels.

Above Caub rises in solemn majesty the castle of Gutenfels.

About the middle of the 13th century Philipp of Falkenstein inhabited it with his sister Guta, who is described as a very beautiful lady, endowed with the noblest qualities of mind and body.

The knight of Falkenstein and his sister were present at a tournament at Cologne, where there was a great assembly of beauty.

Guta, one of the loveliest, soon attracted the attention of all the knights and especially one among them, whose looks always met hers with a lively expression of admiration and tenderness. The knight, who kept his eyes continually fixed upon her and who had made a deep impression upon her heart, was splendidly armed from top to toe and mounted on a spirited horse, the movements of which indicated, that it was high bred.

Nobody recognized him, for his visir was lowered and he had been admitted into the tilt-yard only by a word from the archbishop, whose guest he was.

He advanced into the court and Gutta perceived with interest and pleasure the dexterity, with which the knight managed his wild and fiery steed. The eyes of the knight met hers and with a throbbing heart and blushing cheeks she turned her eyes away in sweet confusion.

With a crash the two knights met each other; Guta dared not lift her eyes up, till a shout of joy announced the victory.

The vanquished was lifted up by the herald and the unknown conqueror rode round the tilt-yard as is the custom. Arrived opposite Guta, he lowered his lance and the maid, surprised by this mark of politeness and in a charming confusion let her glove fall to the ground. The knight picked it quickly up and begged her to present him with it, as a reward of his victory.

Guta could not refuse the gallant knight, he instantly fixed the glove on his helmet, as a sign of the victory which he had gained.

Falkenstein, flattered by the homage paid to his sister, invited the knight, to call upon him in his castle; the stranger accepted the invitation with thanks and withdrew bowing to the lovely

15

Guta; she pressed her hand to her bosom, as if to keep back the violence of her feeling.

Some days after this a knight, accompanied by two servants, entered the castle and was received heartily by Falkenstein.

When the guest was alone with Guta, whose brother had withdrawn for some hours, he turned the conversation upon the tournament and spoke with enthusiasm of the deep impression, which she had made on his heart. Guta listened with lively interest and a heaving bosom to the words of the stranger; only her tears and a tender squeeze of the hands betrayed, that the arrow of the winged God had deeply sunk into her heart.

The avowal of her love had thoroughly changed Guta, renowned before for her haughtiness and pride. Now weak and humble she leant on the knight's breast and his lips met hers in passionate tenderness, while in her half-shut eyes sparkled tears of joy.

When the trambling of her brother's horse was heard in the court-yard, she withdrew from her lover's arms and tried to conceal her confusion as much, as she could.

The knight seized Guta's hand, looking at her with a regard of true and sincere love and saying in a low voice:

„Forgive me, beloved one, to have elicited

the secret of your heart, without the hope of success in demanding your hand from your brother. But wait some months and I shall present myself in my true character and adorned with all the marks of my rank, never to leave you again!"

„I shall be faithful to you till death!" exclaimed she sighing and withdrew, to avoid the scrutinizing regards of her brother.

A war had broken out in Germany on account of a new emperor's election. One party was for Richard of Cornwallis, the other for Alphonse of Castile! the first prince prevailed and was crowned at Frankfort o. M.

Falkenstein, who had sided with Richard, returned to the castle, where Guta waited calmly and confidently for the return of her lover. But after some months had passed, without getting any news of him, she began to despair and her rosy cheeks grew more and more pale and she shut herself in her room to weep and pray.

The brother thought her sick and left her alone, as nothing could appease her grief.

One summer-morning the sun had risen with unusual brilliancy, brightening by her golden-rays the dewy valley and playing on the waves of the river and on the windows of the castle, which appeared, as if they were on fire.

All were happy in the castle as well, as in

the small villages around. Gray columns of smoke mounted in the air. The labourer walked with hasty steps towards the mountains which were covered with vine-yards, while a boy with flaxen hair and bare feet drove the cows towards the pasture.

Nicely dressed girls walked to the castle, with baskets on their fair heads, cheering the way by telling their innocent love-adventures of yesterday or laughing merrily on account of some witty jocund remark of their companions. There suddenly appeared on the road along the Rhine a troop of cavaliers, whose armour and arms shone brilliantly in the sun. They rode a full gallop through the village, the inhabitants of which regarded the splendid troop, with astonishment and wonder who travelled towards Chaube, the lord of which, informed by the sentinel of the tower, received them at the gate.

„God be with thee, noble knight!“ exclaimed the most distinguished of the troop, offering his hand to Falkenstein.

„Be welcome! my king; alight and come in!“ replied the surprised and joyful knight.

Richard lept from his horse and shaking the knight's hand, once more he entered the castle with him.

„Where is your lovely sister knight?“ asked the king merrily.

„Forgive that she has not yet appeared; but she is ill and indulging in her grief!"

„Bring her the message, that king Richard begs her hand; that may cure her and cheer her up."

„I doubt it; for Guta has high sentiments and even a crown would not dissuade her from her resolution. She won't marry and has already rejected many wooers. Howewer, out of love for you, I will ask her once more."

Falkenstein withdrew and Richard walked restlessly to and fro in the apartment. Guta's brother returned instantly and hastening towards the king, said to him:

„I have told her; and she is immoveable!"

„God be praised!" exclaimed the king sighing and his breast seemed to be rid of a heavy burden. „Know, lord of Falkenstein", said he smilling, „that your sister and myself swore fidelity after the tournament of Cologne. I was unknown to you and departed some time after with the promise to return soon and ask for your siter's hand. Obliged to perform my duty at the court, I could not accomplish my promise; but now I appear, to fetch my betrothed, who refused a king to remain faithful to her lover. Take this glove and bring it to her. Tell her, that a knight of the king's train, sent her this sign; lead her hither, that I may congratulate her and accomplish my promise".

Falkenstein took the glove gratefully and went to his sister; no sooner had the maid recognized the glove, than she hastened down and embraced her lover tenderly, with tears of joy.

"You remained faithful to me, dear maid", said the king, pressing her to his breast, "as I remained faithful to you!"

Guta looked at him with a sweet smile, her heart filled with rapture.

"Would I deserve to become emperor of Germany, if I did not profit of the liberty, to keep my word?"

Guta trembled for joy and pressing him tenderly to her bosom, exclaimed with sparkling eyes:

"You? Emperor?"

"Our emperor Richard, your husband!" replied the brother, down whose cheeks tears were flowing.

The marriage ceremony was performed and the emperor Richard took his illustrious consort with him, changing the name of Chaube for Gutenfels, as the castle is denominated to this day.

Schönberg.

n the now decayed castle of Schön-
berg lived in olden times seven sisters,
who were called the seven beautiful
countesses.

The renown of their beauty as well as their
fortune allured from far and near a great many
admirers. Their attentions grew so troublesome
to the seven „beauties", that they a last resolved
to get rid of them.

They made it known, that all, who demanded
their hands' should appear in the castle. The
wooers flocked thither in great numbers, to try
their chance. They were received with courtesy
and when all were assembled, a waiting-woman
brought a silver-vase, filled with little rolls of
parchment, on which were painted the different
colours of the seven ladies.

Each one put his hand into the vase and took
a roll out of it, the result was that the seven
most ugly among them gained and all others
drew blanks.

The jealousy, anger and ironical remarks of the one and the bustling of the others are beyond power of description. The general alarm pre-vented them hearing the peals of laughter, issu-ing from the adjoining room, and the mocking remarks of the seven countesses.

The knights, who had been favoured by fortune demanded to see their future wives and were led solemnly into a saloon, where hung the full-lenght portraits of the seven sisters.

„See, gallant knights, your brides'" exclaimed the maid tittering and making a reverence to the confused lovers, who fled out of the room, breath-ing vengeance.

On the Rhine they saw the lovely maids in a boat adorned with flowers; they were going to another castle. Merrily they laughed and waved their handkerchiefs to the lovers.

The boatmen, who rowed them to the other side of the Rhine, named the seven rocks, which are to be seen at low water, the „seven virgins": but history tells us, that the seven countesses dit not remain so cold and prudish, for many brave and gallant knights were their descendants.

Lurley.

t is no wonder, that there are so many popular tales about the rock of the „Lurley" for there it not a mountain so romantically situated and so interesting.

In times of yore a charming „undine" had selected this rock for her abode; every evening she sate at the top of it, combed her golden hair or accompanied her pathetic and melodius songs on a golden lute.

Every one, who saw and heard her, was charmed and felt in his heart a deep and passionate love, so that for the purpose of seeing the lovely enchantresse, a great many boats, approaching too near the rock, where dashed on it and hurled in the foaming waves.

But the charming „undine" was not always dangerous; for she often rendered men services and she seemed especially to favour the fishermen of the neighbourhood, in showing them from time to time the places, which abounded in fishes.

The renown of her beauty as well, as of her amiability and charity soon spread along the Rhine and allured the son of the „Pfalzgraf" to come and see her. He did not care for the admonitions and warning of some old boatmen, but lept into a boat and bade them steer towards the rock.

The boatmen sighing and shrugging their shoulders obeyed the young counts orders. The boat rapidly crossed the waves, which dashed foaming on towards the rock.

Dark clouds veiled the bright moon and reflected their shadows on the waves, while the summit of the Lurley was illuminated by a silver light, which reflected over the valley of Fluthen.

The young count bent forwards looking with wild and anxious gaze first to the rock and then to the river, in the hope of seeing her. But nothing appeared and discouraged he was about to withdraw.

The boat was already returning, when a charming melody issuing, as it seemed, from the depht of the river, reached his ear. The waves rose with a roaring noise and carried the boat violently away and pushed it towards the rock. There the young man saw with rapture the glorious form of a virgin, clad in a snow-white gown and covered with a sort of green veil.

„There! There! I must and will climb up the rock!" cried the youth, with expressions of wild and passionate love.

The boatmen warned him at first of the danger, to which he would expose himself by this, but irritated by the contradiction he drew his sword and threatened to stab them, if they did not obey. The boatmen sadly seized the oars and rowed towards the rock. The young man, having no more command of himself, lept out of the boat and fell into the foaming waves. The boatmen in vain tried to rescue him; they sought for his corpse, but he remained buried in the Rhine.

At this news his father was seized with violent despair and resolved to take vengeance. He despatched soldiers, to take the sorceress prisoner, for he wished to burn her as a witch.

The men, led by the captain, repaired to the rock and perceived from afar the undine, who looked smilingly at the waves. They climbed the rock cautiously and surrounded it.

„Halloh, sorceress!" — exclaimed the captain, brandishing his naked sword. „The seducing tricks, by which you charmed the young count, have no power over us! Come down, or I shall hurl you into the river!"

Fearlessly she bent down and said with a smile on her rosy lips:

„The Rhine will receive me, which will be better!"

„Nonsense, nonsense! Take care! I shall fetch you!" and saying so he climbed up the rock, on which the „undine" awaited him with a sweet and childish smile.

When the man had arrived there quite exhausted and out of breath and was about to touch her, the „nymph" bent towards the Rhine singing:

> „Hasten hither, lovely waves",
> „Take me quickly to your caves!"

Suddenly a frightful thunderstorm raged round the rock and hurled the captain down. The Rhine foamed like the sea: two immense waves took the fair undine and carried her with them.

The captain rose at last with trembling limbs and chattering teeth and cursing the undine; he returned to follow his men, who had already fled, for it seemed to them, as if they heard thousand of voices screaming to them and the war-cry of a numerous army, marching after them.

With grief and sadness the „palsgraf" saw his want of power. From that time the undine was never seen again.

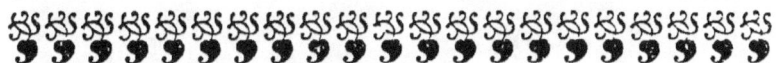

Lurley.

ildly dance the seething waves
And throw their spray around;
There the mists rise from the caves,
Which there about abound.

Sluggishly they twist and twine
Themselves in ghostly forms;
— Seem to guard their fav'rite Rhine
Like phantoms o'er their tombs,

Boatmen, as they near the place,
With fear and moisten'd eye,
Beg most earnestly for grace —
— And Pity from on high.

My son sank here — an old man said,
(His tears began to flow)
Lurline call'd him to the dead;
— Unto her hosts below.

That word „Lurline" echoed round,
And back it slowly came;
Then from the dephts seem'd to sound
In chorus that dread name.

Mayence, 5th July 1875.

John B. Schott.

Lorelay.

esides the foregoing tradition of the fair waternymph another is related, which has likewise reference to the rock called the „Lurley".

There was once to be seen at Bacharach a maid of such exquisite beauty, that every one seeing her became enamoured.

But her virtue and maidenlike timidity protected her against all forwardness; and only one succeeded in gaining her favours, but he had departed for Palestine, to gain laurels and make himself renowned, before he led the fair maid home as his bride.

She was an orphan and every one thought it therefore permitted to try his chance with the maid. As every one was jealous of the other and viewed in him a happier rival, a great many duels were fought and even assassinations were committed. The maid lived in the greatest retirement and was not to be seen any more at church and not even at her window.

It seemed, as if the young men became still more inflamed by the reserve and coyness of the maid. The maid was thought to be possessed of a magical power and this belief was still more confirmed by some priests and monks who had likewise, so report said, tried to gain her favour. The maid was arrested and accused as a sorceress. The archbishop of Cologne, to whom the case was committed as lawful judge in spiritual matters, repaired instantly to Bacharach, to see the maid and to decide according to his own perception. He soon understood the odious motives of the accusers, punished them and consoled the disconsolate maid for the injury inflicted upon her.

„I shall bring you to a place, where your beauty will be secure against persecutions. There you may wait quietly for the return of your beloved or in case of his death, take the veil!"

He ordered three knights, to convey her to a convent and pay every attention to her on the way.

Lorelay fell thankfully at the archbishop's feet and kissed his gown; she then rose and followed her guides.

Arrived at the rock of „Lurley" she went to the top, to take a parting-look at the Rhine and its beautiful banks. Her gaze was directed attentively to a boat, which was at some distance from her. It approached nearer and nearer and she recognized the colours of her lover's flag, who was in the boat. The guides hastened to her, attracted by her joyful shout's; they perceived the boat and rejoiced with the maid, who now wept with joy and fell on her knees, extending her arms towards her lover.

At lenght the boat came so near, that the passengers could be recognized. A splendidly dressed knight stood on the deck and waved his hat. He perceived the people on the rock and among them he recognized his beloved, who made signs to him, which he tenderly and joyfully returned. The boat approached the rock and as all eyes were turned upwards, nobody thought of the wirl-pool, which lurked for its prey and swallowed all that it could seize. The boat was caught by it and slung with such violence against the rock, that it broke.

A cry of terror was heard, the boat disappeared beneath the waves with all hands. The spectators on the rock were filled with horror and especially the maid, who with looks of despair regarded the waves, which had buried her happiness.

Just then a pale face with flaxen hair floating
in disorder rose to the surface of the water.
A frightful cry broke from the lips of the maid
as she plunged down into the river on the corpse
of her lover. The bodies were found later in a
close embrace.

This event still more confirmed the belief in
the waternymph of the „Lurley“.

St. Goar.

ear St. Goar is a chain of rocks which is known by the name of the „bank“; it is very dangerous for fishermen.

Under Sigbert, son of Clotar, king of France, the fishermen lived separately on the banks of the Rhine. They had repaired especially to those parts on account of the quantity of salmon, which abounded there.

The poorer class of people in that time were ignorant and savage, more heathenish than christian; therefore it was a great advantage to them when such a man as Goar came and took up his abode amongst them; for he was a good and true christian. He established himself on one of the most dangerous parts of the Rhine, namely near the „bank“.

He regarded it as his duty to exercise hospitality, to alleviate the misery of the poor, to teach true christianity and especially to help all, who had been shipwrecked at that spot.

Now it is not to be wondered, that the fishermen of the neighbourhood believed him a messenger of heaven and respected and loved him
accordingly.

Through the slander of a prelate, king Sigberts
attention was drawn to the modest life of the
hermit, whom the priests looked upon with jealousy. But Sigbert, who knew how to value him,
recognized his noble principles and as Goar refused every ecclesiastical dignity, the king sent
him rich presents. The king was always favourable to the hermit and when he died, he recom-
mended his cell and tomb to the royal protector
who ordered him to be buried by the priest and
a chapel to be erected over it.

The chapel became a place of pilgrimage and
was gradually altered into a convent, the monks
of which exercised the duties of humanity and
hospitality, by which Goar had done so much
good in his life-time.

Later on a band of robbers plundered and
burnt the church. The count of Arnheim ordered
it to be rebuilt and enclosed by walls. By degrees the town of St. Goar was built around
the convent.

The tomb of the hermit became splendid and
miraculous. Charles the great, who one day
passed before it, without taking any notice of it
was enveloped by such a thick fog, that he was

obliged to pass the night in the open air and only after having returned and said a prayer in the chapel, the fog disappeared and he could continue travelling. His sons Charles and Pipin, whom hatred had set at variance, met by chance at Goar's tomb and where reconciled. His wife Fastrada was cured there of a severe illness, and the emperor built a court and a new church, out of gratitude for all the benefits bestowed by the Saint on his family.

Rheinfels, the cat and the mouse.

After the extinction of the counts of Arnheim, the protectorship of the town of St. Goarshausen devolved on the counts of Katzenellenbogen. The castle of Rheinstein, built in former times and well fortified, became the residence of the new protectors.

The counts of Katzenellenbogen were the neigbours of the archbishop Cuno of Falkenstein and always at variance with the proud and valiant prelate, who endeavoured to extent his dominion to the prejudice of his neighbours.

The counts of Katzenellenbogen, having heard that Cuno had fortified his castle of Thurmberg rebuilt the castle of Neu-katzenellenbogen, which is situated on the right bank of the Rhine and gave it the name of the „cat" and Thurmberg was called the „mouse".

The two fortresses, situated opposite each other, dominated the Rhine, but the castle of Neu-katzenellenbogen barred the passage to the prelate from the upper side of the Rhine. In spite of all their endeavours to catch the „mouse“, Cuno understood how to counteract the tricks and leaps of the cat and keep the mouse unhurt.

The last descendant of the family of Katzen-ellenbogen had a morose and quarrelsome wife, who disturbed the domestic happiness and even ill-treated her own children, a son and daughter. The count was divorced from his wife on acount of her bad and disagreeable charakter and married in later time his son to a maid of the family of Dillenburg-Nassau and his daughter to a member of the family of the „Landgraven“ of Hessen.

Soon after his wedding the young count departed with his uncle John of Nassau for the Netherlands, to take possession of the estates, which fell to his share as the dowry of his wife.

He was stabbed at Bruges in Flanders in the year 1454.

His father, who thus lost the last of his family in the person of his son, resolved to marry again and chose the widow of the duke Otto of Bruns-wick, a young and virtuous lady.

But the relations, who already regarded the count's estates as their property, conspired against the union and bribed the chaplain of the count, to poison the young wife; the priest offered her blessed wine, into which he had thrown arsenic, but the countess, disgusted by the odour of the poisoned wine, drank but very little and that only not to displease the holy man.

She was seized with violent convulsions and could only be saved with much difficulty, but the assiduous care of her old husband accelerated her recovery.

The assassin, pursued by the count of Nassau, father of the victim, was arrested at Cologne and burnt alive at the foot of the gallows, without having however betrayed his accomplices.

The counts sick wife recovered indeed, but without hope of descendants; and after her death the immense estates went to the relations.

The landgrave of Hessen inherited St. Goar and the castle of Rheinfels.

In the year 1692 the Hessian capitain Görz defended the castle successfully against marshall Tallard. But they surrendered in the year 1794 at the first summons of the French, who demolished the fortifications.

The brothers.

o tradition, excepting that of the Lurley is more popular, than the tradition of the two castles Liebenstein and Sternberg, belonging to two brothers.

Dietrich of Liebenstein, who was already in possession of the castle of Sternberg had two sons, whom he educated with a young orphan-maid of the family of Brömser, who was under his guardianship.

The father saw with pleasure, that his sons courted the young and rich heiress, for he was interested in seeing one of his sons married to the orphan, that her inheritance might be joined to the estates of Liebenstein.

After the father's death the brothers and the orphan lived some time together in friendly intercourse, but as the elder one, who was of a grave character, remarked, that the maid favoured more his lively, gay and affectionate brother, he desisted from courting her and favoured their union.

Pilgrims arrived at the banks of the Rhine relating to the people all the wonders of distant countries and priests preached the cross and demanded the knights in the name of Christ to fight for the possession of the Holy Sepulchre, and the destruction of the infidels.

The elder knight, notwithstanding his love for his brother felt a great oppression on his heart and spirits, when he saw the maid jesting tenderly with his brother; so he resolved to take the cross.

But the younger knight was first to form this resolution and one day made it known to them. His brother and his betrothed were alarmed by the hasty vow of the young knight, but the religious enthusiasm prevailed over their consternation and the young crusader took leave of his brother and of his beloved, to whom he vowed fidelity.

„You precede me“, said the elder brother to the young one, „but, though you do wrong, I cannot be angry with you on that account; don't forget your betrothed nor me, who must remain here to guard the castle. Don't forget us and return soon.“

The maid with anxious and tearful eyes watched her lover depart and waved her handkerchief as long as she could see him, but when at a turning of the road he disappeared, she fell sobbing on the breast of his brother, who tried to console her.

The knight had to undergo a hard struggle on account of his daily intercourse with the lovely maid, but he triumphed over the temptation and betrayed neither by looks, nor by any gesture the torments of his heart.

Many months passed thus, when suddenly at the castle of Liebenstein the surprising news arrived, that the younger brother had returned to his castle Sternberg; at the same time the rumour spread, that a Grecian maid of high beauty had come with him, as his wife. At this news the unhappy maid fell senseless to the ground, while the elder knight strode furiously up and down the apartment and shed tears of rage and grief.

His brother at the castle of Sternberg dispatched a messenger to Liebenstein with a letter, in which he proffered excuses, but the brother tore it to pieces without having read it and said to the messenger:

„Tell your perfidious master, that every intercourse between us is broken for ever and that I shall have revenge for his crime!“

Saying this he gave the messenger his glove and challenged his brother.

The day of the unnatural duel at length arrived. The brothers repaired armed to the borders of their estates and had already drawn their swords, when a soft voice commanded them to stop. The maid stepped, like a guardian-angel, between the combatants, regarding them with imploring looks.

„Dear brother“, said she to the elder one in a soft tune, mingled with reproach, „would you, for my sake, pollute your hand by the brother's blood? No, that you will not, you love me too much and will not increase my misery by a murder; but you,“ continued she turning to the younger one, who was half contrite, „you, who have broken your vows to me, be as happy in the arms of the Grecian lady, as you can be. I forgive you and shall pray for you in the couvent.“

She then withdrew as softly as she had come and abandoned the brothers to their grief.

„Forgive“, exclaimed the younger one sobbing, „forgive me, my dear brother; overpowered by passion I have grievously offended you and that angel.“

He knelt down suppliantly and offered his brother his hand and then threw away his sword. The features of the elder one now brightened and not able, any longer to master his feelings, he embraced the brother and pressed him to his breast.

The seconds, who had stood with anxious

expectation rejoiced at the reconciliation and embraced each other also.

The sun, who had been veiled before by a gray mist, re-appeared again and threw its brilliant rays over the fields.

The elder brother tried to dissuade the maid from her resolution, proposing to her, to remain with him as his wife, but she replied, that she could not devote to another man a crushed and wronged heart and that she would find no rest, but in a convent.

He complied with a bleeding heart and accompanied her himself to the convent, which she had chosen.

The infidelity of the younger brother was punished. His frivolous wife yielded to the seductions of another, became faithless and fled with her seducer.

From this time the two brothers lived happily together. To honour the grievously injured nun they remained unmarried and their only pleasure was, to visit each other frequently and pass some hours in each other's company.

Boppard.

This once free and imperial town, which like many other towns along the Rhine is now no longer in its grandeur and splendour, was in the Roman times called Bodobriga and possessed a castle of the kings of France, the ruins of which are still to be seen.

In the reign of Frederick the first, there lived in the above mentioned town an enterprising, humorous and brave fellow. namend Conrad, a descendant of the noble family of „Bayer of Boppard". He courted a noble maid of the neighbourhood, whom he was resolved to marry after the return of her brother, who had gone to Palestine with the crusaders, under the command of Frederick the I.

Robbers profited by the emperor's absence, to plunder the castles and towns. And Conrad had to suffer many attacks from them, and after having repulsed them, he succoured other knights

who were in the same danger, only to satisfy
his desire for combat.

By this adventurous and warlike life his love
for his betrothed, Maria, gradually cooled. He
neglected her and at lenght broke his promise
at the same time by sending her a letter, containing the resignation of her hand.

But no sooner had he dispatched this message,
than he repented it and reproached himself.

To silence the voice of his conscience, he
tried to divert his mind by drinking, but that
was of no avail. He mounted his horse, accompanied by some cavaliers and departed for the
chase

The valley and the neighbouring forest was
covered with the morning dew. It fell in drops
from the flowers and the foliage of the trees,
and glittered in the rays of the sun. Every
thing seemed more beautiful than usual. The
knight rode joyfully on and entered the forest
with his companions. The dogs sprang round
the neighing horses. But soon their howling
announced that a track had been found.

The chase became wilder. The stag had
made an opening in a thick foliage and disappeared in an underwood: the dogs pursued it.
But Conrad, finding the wood too thick, took
another path. Listening at the same time attentively to the dog's barking which suddenly died

away, he found with anger, that he had lost the right path and had left the hunting-ground far behind him.

Fatigued and discontented he stopped his horse to repose a little and then to rejoin the chase; but his intention was baffled by the appearance of an armed knight, who stopped before him and challenged him to a combat.

„Ah, rash being“, exclaimed Conrad foaming with fury, „have you such an eager desire to die? Who are you? Up, with your visir!“

„Not at all, Conrad!“ replied a soft voice „I challenge you in Maria's name, whose brother I am!“

The anger on account of the chase, the reproach of his conscience and the unexpected challenge made Conrad furious; he turned his horse and rushed with naked sword at his adversary. His adversary sunk down from his horse, covering his bosom with his hands, from which the blood ran copiously.

Seized by a sad foreboding Conrad hastened to the vanquished to take off his helmet. But how great was his terror, when he recognized in the eyes lifted up to him those of his beloved Maria, whom he had so shamefully abandoned and who now expired in his arms, giving him a look of love and forgiveness.

Furious and in a state of madness he threw

himself on the ground near the corpse, tore his hair and uttered curses against himself and his criminal deed. When his paroxysm was over, he knelt before his beloved and wept long and bitterly. It was night, when Conrad left the corpse and returned home.

He arrived at Boppard pale and disfigured and all who saw him or were about to salute him, drew back, frightened by his distracted and terrible expression.

Without speaking to anybody, he left the town on the following day and as he did not return, his servants sought through his apartment, where they found his last will, by which he had devoted his fortune to the erection of a convent on the site of Maria's tomb.

Nobody knew, where Conrad had retired. Only after many years it was reported, that he had become one of the bravest and most daring templers and that he had been the first in the assault of Ptolomais, and who planted the christian flag on the battlements. But in doing so he fell pierced by an arrow.

Lahneck.

Below Boppard, where the Lahn flows into the Rhine, on one of the mountains that border it, is the fortress of Lahneck, which through the last defeat of the order of Templars bears a sorrowful celebrity.

It belonged to the Templars, who fortified it. A house of their order was to be found in every large town and especially near the Rhine.

The order of the knight Templars was founded in 1118 by Godfrey of Bouillon for the protection of pilgrims and the defence of the Holy sepulchre. In a short time the order became renowned and spread all over the world. It was also an immensely rich order and was therefore envied and disliked by the clergy.

Clemens the 5th, whose politics were hostile to the Templars, was aided by Philip „le bel" and made an alliance with the king, to destroy the power of the order by a political stratagem.

According to this plan the grand-master Molay with sixty French knights was invited to a consulation and when they arrived, they were perfidiously arrested, led before a tribunal, consisting of monks and priests and accused of heresy. After an imprisonment of many years, they were condemned to be burnt alive; the sentence was executed on the 18th March 1324 and the grand-master eighty years of age with sixty knights perished in the flames. When the grand-master mounted the pile of wood, he lifted up his hand to heaven and exclaimed with a hollow and trembling voice: „In the name of the Holy Trinity I summon our murderers before the tribunal of God, to give account of the‘ crime, which they are now about to commit. May God have mercy on us.“

The Templars died, but the summons was heard above, for in the same year the pope and the king died.

Except in France, no other personal injustice was inflicted on the order. The pope abolished it with seizure of their properties, the greater part of which fell to the share of ecclesiastical orders, but that was only the case in France.

At this time lived Peter of Aichspalt, who occupied the archiepiscopal see of Mayence and as a favourite of the pope, he thought himself likewise obliged to oppress the Templars. He ordered the knights to leave his dominions and threatened to expel them by force, if they did not depart. A great number of them obeyed, abjured their vow and sought their sustenance and welfare elsewhere. Some of the bravest threw themselves into the fortress of Lahneck and defied the summons of the archbishop. who sent troops, to drive them away. The knights fought valiantly and even, when their commander fell, they despised the summons to surrender and replied with contempt to the messengers, who exhorted them to lay down their arms. All perished expected one, who defended the entrance of the fortress.

The besiegers wanted to spare him and granted him time for consideration. Then they summoned him, to surrender, but he replied with a proud, daring refusal, pointing to his fallen brethren. The combat was about to begin again, but at this moment a messenger arrived in haste, and proclaimed a truce in the name of the emperor. They laid down their arms respectfully and the messenger addressed the last of the heroes saying:

„Surrender to me your arms, noble knight; I regret, to have arrived to late for the deliverance of your brethren, but to the last of the brave I can offer safety for his life and property".

17*

„Think of Molay and his murdered companions; look at my fallen comrades,“ replied the Templar proudly, „I know no mercy, for as they perished, so will I!“

Saying this, he rushed on the surprised enemy and pierced with wounds fell near his fallen brethren.

Stolzenfels.

It was a stormy night, the rain poured down in torrents and the wind howled frightfully around the battlements of Stolzenfels, when a pilgrim knocked at the gate and was admitted by the treasurer of the archbishop, Werner of Falkenstein.

The pilgrim's name was Maso, and he was a thin, gloomy looking man, whos dark beard flowed down to his waist and gave his face the expression of deep thought, bearing a strange contrast to the malicious and cunning expression of his eyes.

In those times there were many, who studied Alchemy, Astrology and Magic, but particularly the first.

Werner of Falkenstein, like his treasurer, followed this art and many pieces of gold they sacrificed to the crucible, but without any result. The pilgrim was admitted after having announced himself learned in the art of Alchymy.

The treasurer prepared a room in one of the towers and passed whole nights with him there. He had a daughter, who grew in all the beauty of maiden loveliness and who was the only comfort of her father. She saw with secret anxiety the power the pilgrim had over her father and with pain and sorrow she perceived a great change in him. He now took no notice of her endearments and shut himself up in the room more than usual and when he left it, it was with dejected and gloomy looks.

One day a messenger arrived at the castle with the news that the archbishop with some noblemen and knights were coming to remain a few days.

With horror Elisabeth saw the impression this news made on her father, for he turned deadly pale and staggered back some paces and with difficulty resumed his wonted composure. Soon after this she perceived him striding hastily up and down his apartment, beating his forehead and weeping. She was about to rush in and try to comfort him, when he suddenly and with a frightful cry of despair fled into the mysterious room, the door of which he locked.

The maid, driven by anguish, followed her father and remained stupefied at the door, hearing him uttering complaints and bitter reproaches. She could hardly suppress the scream of despair,

that was rising to her lips and with tottering
limbs and aching head she leaned against the
wall pressing her hands to her bosom. A grave
and steady voice replied to the violent reproaches
of the treasurer saying:

„Bring hither a pure and stainless virgin,
whose heart never knew love for man and you
shall have gold. It is only your obstinacy, that
made you fail till now!“

Impostor! Wretch! Shall I pollute my hands
by a murder?“ exclaimed the treasurer. „I have
melted down my fortune and honour and abused
the confidence of my master and should I more-
over shed innocent blood! Cursed be your de-
luding art! Give me my gold or I shall strangle
you with my own hands!“

„Only the heart's blood of a virgin can
suffice; however if you wish it, I will try once
more!“

„Try! Try! I must have gold, and if I should
go to perdition for it!“

He then withdrew hastily, to cool his anger
in the open air.

The alchemist looked after him with a sardonic
smile, which however soon disappeared, for he
saw before him Elisabeth pale and her eyes filled
with tears.

„I have heard all and I am the virgin, who

for her father's sake, will sacrifice her life and blood!"

Inflamed by his wild desire the pilgrim regarded her with covetous looks, but beeing master of the art of dissembling, he suddenly changed and became amiable and tender and was about to take her hand.

She started back shuddering.

„Don't touch me!" exclaimed she. „Your contact is profanation. Tell me, what I must do and I will run the dagger with my own hands into my breast!"

The pilgrim turned away and an expression of revenge played about his features: he replied:

„Return hither at midnight; I shall prepare the crucible for that hour and your father at sun-rise will have abundant riches and honour."

„Can you swear that on the cross?"

The monk took out a little crucifix from his breast, turned towards her and said in a grave and solemn tone:

„If you obey me and do every thing I tell you, I swear that your father will become rich and honoured."

„I shall come!" replied the maid with a light sigh withdrawing.

The monk looked after her with a malicious smile, „Do you think to delude me, little dove!"

Die Büßerin

said he murmuring. „I shall tame you, in spite
of the cross, which has already rendered me
excellent services!" and with a mischievous smile
he pressed a secret spring and a dagger sprang
forth.

„A lucky thought", said he, „to join these
two together! Hell in alliance with heaven!"

In deep thought he replaced the dagger into
its sheath and concealed the cross on his breast.
Then he shut himself in, entered the adjoining
room and loosened with a crow-bar a square stone
from the floor. With a triumphant air he lifted
up a leather-bag, opened it and let the pieces
of gold, which it contained, glide with rapture
through his fingers.

„That is the secret of making gold!" said
he. „The fools seek it in the crucible, but wise
men know to take advantage of the harvest-time!
Come, my friends, whe shall to-day find an opportunity of escape! The maid shall open my
cell and with day-break I shall be in safety,
before they think of pursuing."

During this soliloquy he fastened the leathern
belt around his waist, replaced the stone and
waited the night, which should be wittness of
his shameful crime and flight!

During this interval was a great stir and
activity in the castle, the servants and knights
entered with the baggage of the archbishop and

unsaddled the foaming horses admist talking and laughing; in the apartments the women were occupied in cleaning.

Elisabeth pale and sad superintended the servants and surveyed their work; her father, who had returned from the alchymist with new hope now made the necessary arrangements for the reception of his sovereign, and when Elisabeth met him, he pressed her, full of love and hope on his breast and kissed her. He did not know, how vain his hopes were and seized like a drowning man at a straw.

The archbishop soon made his appearance and the guns of welcome told he was near; he came with a brilliant train and the inmates of the castle hailed him with loud shouts. He replied to the salutations with kindness, and having alighted, he squeezed the hand of the treasurer. Arrived in the castle he expressed his wish to see Elisabeth and when her father presented her, he addressed the maid amicably:

„Eh, how you have grown and I fear, that your beauty will fascinate many a heart!"

Then he turned towards his knights with a jesting warning and presented them to her and many tender looks were directed to the maid, who blushing dared not lift her eyes.

After some kind adresses the archbishop withdrew and entered his apartment. The young girl unable longer to restrain her tears, retired to her room and deplored her unhappy fate.

Among the knights was a descendant of the family of Westerburg, on whom the appearance of the beautiful girl had made a deep impression; her image was always before his eyes and caused him a sleepless night.

The moon shone and the nightingale warbled in the surrounding bushes. The knight stood at the window and looked down in the court-yard, where a deep silence reigned; he could see a part of the treasurer's apartments, one of which was inhabited by Elisabeth.

The treasurer had bid his daughter good-night more tenderly than usual.

„You are a good girl", said he, carressing her cheeks, „I shall be to-morrow as merry and kind as ever and delivered from the night-mare, which oppresses my heart!"

He withdrew sighing to his apartment, in which he strode up and down in great excitement.

The hour, at which Elisabeth should repair to the pilgrim, approached.

She with a resolute air, seized the candle and went hastily to the alchymist, who at her entrance rose, laying down his books, in which he had seemed to be absorbed.

The young knight, who watched the window
of Elisabeth's room, perceived with surprise the
light disappear and shortly after the maid walking through the court-yard to the most remote
part of the castle. Impelled by curiosity and
suspecting a mystery he stepped softly down and
advanced towards the place, where Elisabeth had
disappeared. Arrived there he detected a crack
in a door, through which he peeped.

He saw in the pilgrim's apartment the maid
upon her knees, while the alchymist was bent
over a pot, the contents of which he seemed to
examine.

Then you are firmly resolved, to do every
thing, that I shall bid you?" asked he, casting
a triumphant side-look at her.

The maid replied in so low a tone, that the
listener was unable to hear, what she said.

„If that is the case, I will reward your father
and restore the gold, which he took from his
own chest as well as from that of the archbishop.
Honour for honour, blood for blood; thus declares
the sacred book of science. If you sacrifice your
honour, your father shall get honours and his
name become glorious among the knights. If you
sacriflice your blood, I can procure gold, which
will preserve him from infamy. Prepare yourself for the sacrifice, for the spirit tells me, that
your beauty shall not fade away thus!"

The knight perceived, trembling by fear and jealousy, the impudent pilgrim approaching the maid and casting lustful looks at her. He was about to burst open the door, but he desisted, when he heard Elisabeth with a proud and noble air crying:

„Away, impudent wretch! I came to sacrifice my blood for my father's welfare, but I shall suffer no insult, even for his sake!"

The pilgrim turned aside shrugging his shoulders and spoke as if to himself: „I have no time to loose; open your bosom, for the mixture clarifies." He then drew with his little stick a magic circle and uttered some mysterious words, while the maid knelt down praying. Suddenly she seized the dagger, but in the same moment the door flew open and the knight rushed upon her, and disarmed her. The dagger sunk from her hands and she fainted.

The pilgrim stood stupefied at the sight of the young knight. But, while the knight was occupied in assisting the maid, he profited by the opportunity and escaped.

Elisabeth gradually recovered her senses. Like one, haunted by a frightful dream, she tried to recollect herself and after having recognized her situation, she began to sob and shed a flood of tears.

The consoling words of the young man fell,

like balm upon her soul and inspired her with courage and confidence. She confessed to him all, for her heart was oppressed and she wished to discharge it of its load. When she ceased to speak and concealed her face bathed in tears on his breast, he bade her take heart, assuring her that he would assist her father in adversity and procure him the gold which he wanted.

„Be of good heart!" added he, „I rejoice, that a lucky chance has enabled me, to save you. I have found a treasure more estimable, than the alchymist can get.

Elisabeth looked at him with eyes full of tenderness and gratitude and like one subdued by an invisible power, their lips met and they sealed their betrothal by a long and passionate kiss.

The next day the hnight presented himself to the father, who heard with the greatest consternation, what had passed and the escape of the pilgrim, but when the knight confessed his love for Elisabeth, asking her hand and offering him at the same time his purse, the heart of the treasurer swelled and he pressed, with tears of joy, the noble and generous knight to his breast.

The same day fishermen found a corpse in the Rhine, which was instantly recognized as that of the pilgrim. The gold, which was found in his belt, was delivered to the archbishop and as the treasuror sincerely confessed all what had occurred between him and the alchymist, who had misused his confidence, he returned him all the gold, which the treasurer had lost.

Elisabeth received as a reward of her filial love and courage, which she had shown by offering her life as a sacrifice for her father a rich wedding-present and lived happily with her beloved husband to an old age.

———————

Hammerstein.

Count Otto of Hammerstein was the last of that family and with him that illustrious name died in the eleventh century. He was in war with the archbishop of Erkenbold, because the latter had anulled, at the synod of Nymwegen, without the consent of either the counts marriage. The count and his wife Irmengard took little notice of the archbishop's unjust act. But the emperor Henry the second, to whom the clergy gave the surname of the Saint, because he had favoured it in every manner and let himself be guided by the priests, marched with an army against the count, who insisted upon remaining with his wife and not leaving his children. The emperor besieged the fortress, which could only be conquered by famine.

After the death of Otto, Hammerstein fell to the emperor. The emperor gave it to the archbishops of Cologne.

In the year of 1105 the old castellain was sitting in the best room of the castle. Near him at the left side of the high, massive arm-chair of oak, which had become black by age, hung his trusty sword, while at his right sat a noble dog, whose head reposed on the knees of his master. The merry old man had before him on the table a bowl of excellent Rhenish wine, while his two daughters tried to cheer him by their merry, childish love.

„Bring your sister's harp you puss, that she may sing us one of her romances!" exclaimed the father and the lively shild rose quickly, to fetch the instrument which she gave to her dark-eyed and thoughtful sister.

After having tuned it, her delicate fingers ran over the strings and she then accompanied her rich and pathetic voice to the following words:

> Wherefore are your thoughts from here,
> Beloved one tell me why?
> Wherefore in that eye a tear?
> To glory you will fly — ?
>
> Is not the sun as bright to you,
> Are not it's rays as warm?
> Have not the flow'rs a splendid hue,
> And am I not your own?
>
> Restless has your spirit grown,
> So great your thirst for fame;
> Remain where peace you've always known;
> Seek not a hero's name. —

18

„Yes, yes!" said her father sighing, „that is a charming song, but nothwithstanding its beauty, it saddens the heart. It is true, I love you both, but I wish, that you wore jackets instead of petticoats and could manage the sword instead of the spinning-wheel. Indeed, if I had a son, I would be the happiest father."

„And what hinders you, to be so?" said the eldest softly, putting her delicate hands on the large browny fists of her father. He looked tenderly at his charming daughter, whose sweet eyes were fixed on him and as if angry with himself, he cast down his eyes and said sighing:

„You are right, girl! It is folly to desire things we cannot have!"

„Only wait, father!" said the merry fair one, „I will put on a jacket, take a lance and go fighting, like a true knight! You will live, to see my name renowned and at night I will take the lute, stand before the window of my sweetheart and serenade her!" and then she warbled a charming love-song and danced through the room with such a roguish air that a looker on could not have helped admiring her. But she stopped suddenly and listened, for she heard a violent knock at the door. The dog started up barking and growling.

„Two pilgrims, who claim hospitality, are without!" announced the servant.

„Let them enter", said the castellain. „nobody
shall pass by this castle without having refreshed
himself, as long I have a glass of wine and a
bit of bread in store!"

The servant withdrew and opened the gate.
Soon after two strangers entered the apartment,
a young and an old man. The castellain rose
to receive them: but when he approached nearer
and perceived the altered features of the old one,
who let his hood fall back. He fell upon his
knees, exclaiming:

„My lord and emperor!"

„Yes, yes", said Henry (Henry the fourth,
who had escaped from the prison, where his son
detained him by the advice of the archbishops),
„it is your emperor, dear friend, who comes as
fugitive, to claim your hospitality!"

„As fugitive!" cried the castellain with grief
and surprise.

„As fugitive!" repeated the emperor. „an
enemy dared to insult me and imprison an infirm
old man!"

„Ha! Who is the wretch, that dared to commit such a crime against his old and venerable
emperor?" asked the castellain with a loyal
passion and stretching out his hand towards his
sword, which hung by him.

„My son, my own son!" replied the unfortunate father, covering his face with both hands and weeping bitterly.

„Your own son!“ stammered the castellain

„Thank God, brave friend, that you have no sons and that your good daughters cheer your old age. Oh, how joyfull would I change my lot for yours!“

The emperor remained in the castle some days and the castellain accompanied him to Cologne, where other faithful subjects received him. Grief and many humiliations, which he had to endure, soon brought him to the grave.

The castellain often remembered the emperor's words and he wished for nothing more, than to be able to live and enjoy the society of his charming daughters.

———————

Rolandseck & Nonnenwerth.

pposite Drachenfels is the castle of
Rolandseck and below them on an island
in the Rhine, is the convent of Nonnen-
werth.

Roland, a brave knight, nephew of Charles
the great, whose valorous deeds were sung by
the poets, was riding one day for pleasure on
the banks of the Rhine and claimed the hospitality of the lord of Drachenfels.

Scarce had he told his name, than the lord
of the castle, whose exploits were known and
praised in all christendom, came to meet him.

The ladies received the amiable and renowned
guest with as much cordiality as the lord.
Especially the daughter, who looked at him for a
moment and cast down her eyes quickly, as a deep
blush covered her face; the eyes of Roland were
on her with rapture and admiration.

Like one, awaking from a blissful dream,
he obeyed the bidding of the lord, to put off
his armour and even when he was alone in his

own room the image the lovely and modest maid hovered before his eyes.

The hero remained some days in the castle and felt himself more and more fascinated by the maidenly beauty and purity. Happy was he when sitting near her at her work-table he could perceive, with what dexterity her tender fingers managed the needle, and embroidered arabesques or flowers of the most glowing colours on the linen.

Only, when the mother or the maid, especially the latter, with a rash and timid regard, asked him, to relate some tales, the words flowed from his lips. He became eloquent about the lovely countries, where he had lived and combated. Then his cheeks glooved, his eyes sparkled and the maid regarded him with enthusiasm, till his eyes met hers and then she blushingly would resume her work. Roland was roused from this blissful revery by the war, which summoned all the knights away.

Roland could not resist the call of duty, but he recognized with deep grief, what high bliss he must leave behind. With a bleeding heart he went once more to all the favourite places where he had passed such happy moments at her side. An irresistible curiosity drew him towards a bower of honey-suckle, from where loud sobbing was audible. When he had entered, he perceived the beautiful maid sitting on a mossbank weeping bitterly. He knelt down before her and she let her head fall on his shoulder. They spoke not a word; both knew too well, what passed in their hearts. And Roland pressed his beloved to his bosom, kissing away the tears from her eyes

„I shall return“, said he in a low tune, „and we shall then be united for ever.“

The maid did not reply, but Roland understood her silence and pressed her tenderly to his breast. The betrothal was celebrated without any show or splendour and a few days after Roland departed. From time to time they heard reports of glorious victories, which Roland had gained and soon the news of the defeat of the enemy arrived. Bonfires were lighted on the summits of the surrounding hills.

But at Drachenfels silence and sadness reigned, for with the news of the victory arrived likewise that of Roland's death and in the castle were to be seen pale and sad faces and tearful eyes.

As deeply as love had taken root in the maid's heart as deep and intense was her grief, when she heard the news of Roland's death.

Her religious and melancholy charakter gave her consolation in prayer and with the firm belief of meeting her beloved again in heaven, she resolved to wait for that happy moment in a convent.

The parents allowed her, though with regret, to perform her resolution.

Every morning the afflicted parents looked down from the ramparts of their castle into the convent and there saw their daughter, who always waved her hand to them and then withdrew to the chapel.

One day however a joyful activity reigned in the castle, for a troop of knights appeared at the foot of the rock. The gate was opened and Roland joyfully entered with his soldiers, but the smile upon his lips disappeared at once, when he heard, that his betrothed had taken the veil.

„We believed the report of your death true“, said the father, „and suffered her to enter the convent.“

A cry of despair issued from the knight's lips and he covered his face with both hands and allowed his feelings to unman him.

At lenght and as if driven by despair, he mounted on horseback and rode to the oder side of the Rhine.

Opposite to Drachenfels stood the castle of Rolandseck. The hero remained there some weeks and abandoned himself to his grief.

One evening, when he was looking at the convent, he heard the bells tolling and saw a funeral procession of nuns carrying a coffin to the chapel.

With a sad presentiment Roland offered up a prayer and wept bitterly. His page soon after entered and when he perceived his master still weeping, he tried to console him and said softly:

„Sir, the countess of Drachenfels is dead!"

„I know it!" replied Roland. „Saddle my horse and let us depart, so that I may soon join her!"

The knight still performed many brave deeds and at lenght he fell in a combat with the Moors in Spain, attaining the aim, which he so ardently desired.

———

Frederick and Gela.

In the 12th century the fortress near Gelnhausen stood in all its majesty and splendour, where now only ruins are to be seen. It was the favourite residence of the young prince Frederick, a descendant of the emperor Barbarossa, who passed the happiest days of his youth there.

The castellain, a vererable old man, who loved the young prince with fatherly tenderness, had two beautiful and graceful daughters, one of whom, named Gela, had inflamed the heart of the young duke.

One day, meeting the maid and finding himself no longer master of his feeling, he took her hand declared his love and left her abruptly. He passed some days, between fear and hope. All his endeavours to meet his beloved again, were in vain, for she avoided him as much as possible.

Grieved at not having seen Gela and fearing, that he had acted too rashly, he went one afternoon into the fields and was joyfully surprised, to meet the pretty maid gathering flowers.

She was about to run away, but when she perceived the sorrowful mien of the young man, she stopped, offered him her hand and said with down-cast eyes and blushing cheeks:

„I love you, Frederick and I shall wait for you this evening in the church!"

Then she went away, leaving him to his happiness.

In the evening Frederick hastened to the church. Hours passed away, and at last Gela arrived with light steps, sat down at his side and suffered him to press her passionately to his breast. The happy pair felt all the bliss of pure and sincere love.

Many months passed and every night the young lovers met before the altar.

But their happiness was not to continue. The noise of war was heard throughout Germany and many knights were decorated with the cross. Frederick also wished to go with the crusaders. When he communicated his resolution to Gela, she encouraged his desire and told him to depart to gain laurels in the holy war.

Frederick soon after took leave of her and departed.

As an experienced warrior and covered with glory he returned and hastened to meet his beloved Gela, to whom he had been faithful and was now resolved to marry.

But instead of her embraces he received a letter. After having read it, he stood stupified and shed hot tears.

„Frederick", wrote the maid, you are duke and must marry a princess of your own rank. I retire to a convent, to keep my love for you pure and unviolated."

Even when Frederick had been crowned emperor, he did not forget Gela and her sincere love. He carried her letter with him in all his campaigns and it never left his side during his whole life.

In remembrance of the lovely Gela he built the town of Gelashausen, now Gelnhausen.

Drachenfels.

With the flight of thought and on the wings of imagination I lead my reader back to Drachenfels.

The castle is, as we mentioned before, situated on the highest mountain of the „Siebengebirg" and very often the clouds obscure it from the sight.

The following tradition gives us the history of its origin.

Once a wild and terrible dragon inhabited a cavern of the mountain and ravaged the neighbourhood. The consternation and horror, which this monster created in the whole country, was increased by a war, which broke out between the Christian tribes and their heathenish neighbours. But the God of war favoured the heathens and they returned victorious into their country, laden with booty and a great number of prisoners, among whom was a very beautiful maid of noble origin. The chief of the victorious party wished to possess her, but it was especially the good

and humane Ottfried, who had been infatuated
by her beauty. When the booty was being dis-
tributed, every one wanted to possess the maid.
To prevent all quarrel they asked the Priestess
of night to decide the maid's fate.

„If the beauty of the prisoner is such, that
she creates hatred and enmity amongst us, nobody
shall possess her and she must be given to the
dragon!" replied the priestess.

No one dared to oppose this sentence. Ottfried
was deeply moved and seized by despair, when the
maid was led to the cavern, where the dragon was.

The people waited with horror und curiosity,
to see the end of the spectacle.

The maid advanced with firm and resolute
steps towards the cavern, the dragon crept forth
and looked at the frightened maid with his small
eyes; then amidst the cries of the spectators it
rushed on the victim, but suddenly fell, as if
struck by lightning, at her feet.

The crowd was filled with wonder and surprise and the maid stood pale and trembling,
but Ottfried stood before her and had plunged
his sword into the monster, which lay dead at
their feet.

The assembled people shouted with joy, when
they saw, what had happened. All hastened to
the place and carried the maid and her deliverer
in triumph home, where even his rivals congra-

tulated Ottfried for having saved the charming maid by such a courageous deed.

When the multitude had retired, Ottfried asked the still terrified maid:

„What gave you the strenght, to go to meet that monster and to be so firm and courageous, when you saw it? The most valiant trembled at the sight and the bravest men would not have performed, what you a frail, tender woman, did!“

The maid drew a cross from her bosom and presented it to him, saying:

„This cross is the talisman, which makes me strong and courageous, for he, who believes on Him, who hung on it, fears neither death nor grave!“

Ottfried regarded the cross with astonishment but when the maid had explained every thing to him he believed and was baptized.

The maid gave her hand to her deliverer, for whom she felt love and gratitude. Ottfried built the castle of Drachenfels to his wife's honour and made his subjects happy.

Stromberg.

 n his journey to the holy land Diether of Schwarzeneck remained in the castle of Argenfels and became enamoured with Bertha, the youngest and beautiful daughter of the count.

He departed from Argenfels with the firm resolution, that, when he returned, he would marry the lovely maid, whose favour he had gained during his sojourn at Argenfels.

The knight was taken prisoner by the Saracens at Ptolomais.

He passed many tedious and miserable days, thinking of his house and his love. He made a vow, to erect a chapel, if heaven would grant him his liberty.

His fervent prayer was heard. One day his gaolers seemed more busy and alarmed than usual. A clashing of arms was heard, mingled with the Allah of the Moors.

The knight passed some hours in anxious

expectation. At lenght the prison's door opened and a troop of crusaders entered and broke his chains. After his deliverance Dither still fought in many battles and then returned home.

Arrived on the banks of the Rhine he hastened to Argenfels to see his beloved. But instead of the castle he saw with horror nothing but ruins. A shepherd told him, that a band of robbers had attacked, plundered and destroyed the castle.

The boy knew not, what had become of the daughters, but he assured the knight, that they had been saved, as he did not see them among the prisoners.

Sad and dejected Diether went to his castle changed his knight's dress for a pilgrim's coat and travelled in this disguise through the country.

Fatigued and weary after a long journey he arrived one day at a hermitage near Stromberg and resolved to claim the hospitality of the hermit. But what was his surprise, when he perceived instead of a man, a beautiful maid, kneeling before a cross of wood and absorbed in fervent prayer. He stopped respectfully and waited for the conclusion of the prayer. When the maid at lenght rose, he went to meet and salute her; but when he looked at her, he cried with surprise and rapture: „Bertha, my dear Bertha!" and fell at her feet.

Bertha received her lover with kindness and

pressed him to her bosom. Her sister, attracted by the shouts of joy, came and congratulated the knigth.

Diether learnt in the course of the evening that an enemy of their father had profided by the emperor's absence, had attacked Argenfels and burnt it.

Their father had been killed in pursuing the robbers and they had escaped by a subterranean passage and took refuge in the hermitage, where they now were.

After their father's death they had resolved to pass their days in solitude. „But now," interrupted Diether, „you must renounce this plan and follow me to my castle. Bertha, know, that without you I can't live!"

Bertha pressed his hand tenderly and sunk on his breast. But her pious sister declared, that she would remain in the hermitage.

Diether executed his vow and built a chapel on the mountain of Stromberg. But long before it was finished, Bertha became his happy wife. The two lived many years in undisturbed happiness, esteemed and beloved by every one,

Treuenfels.

hoever has travelled through the romantic valleys of the „Siebengebirg“, must know the mountain of Treuenfels, on which is to be seen an altar with the name of „Liba“ on it. The other letters are illegible and the chapel enclosing the altar is now a ruin.

The knight Balther, who possessed a castle in the „Siebengebirg“, had given his daughter Liba to the young knight Schott of Grünstein and waited calmly and happily for the close of his life.

At this time Engelbert I. occupied the episcopal see of Cologne and governed his country with a paternal care and great wisdom. He was very charitable to the poor, amended the laws and favoured the citizenship, by energetically restraining the usurpation of the nobility.

So it was no wonder, that the archbishop was hated as much by the nobility, as he was beloved by the citizens.

Knight Balther, though he was not addicted to robbery, like many of his fellow-knights, still abhorred the arrangements and admonitions of the archbishop and thought the privileges, granted to the citizens, as an insult to the credit and honour of knighthood.

He spoke with harsh words about Engelbert and as his castle was frequented by many visitors, his bitter remarks contributed, to increase the discontentment.

One evening, as he was conversing on the same subject, in the presence of a great many knights, he grew angry about a new decree from the archbishop. Vainly one of the knights contradicted him, representing the great power of the prelate, which could not be resisted. The old man growing more furious exclaimed:

„If you were true men, you would join your forces and make an alliance against this arrogant priest, and stop his presumption. If I had met such a one in my youth, I would have shown him, that knighthood will not suffer to be insulted, but you are insipid individuals and miserable cowards!"

After the old man's angry speech the knights looked down in gloomy silence, as if they seemed to be weighing the chances of so perilous an undertaking. At last a knight rose, took a goblet and cried:

„Friends and noblemen, knight Balther is right; if we made an alliance, we would be powerful enough, to keep this arrogant prelate in check. Those, who are of my opinion, take the goblet and pledge alliance and fidelity against our enemy!

The goblets were filled and lifted; the knights pledged their honour and fidelity, for the words had inflamed all hearts.

The knights after having left the castle of Balther, endered into a conspiracy against the archbishop, waylaid and murdered him one evening, when he was returning from a short journey.

This atrocious deed excited horror and revenge, The assassins were by the emperor's order's persued and arrested. All the inquiries and proofs accused Balther as the chief of the conspirators and the emperor instantly dispatched troops, to take the knight prisoner and demolish his castle.

The troops approached and set fire to the castle before any one was aware of it. Liba hastened to her father, rescued him from the flames and fled with him through a subterranean passage to a thick forest.

There she lived in solitude with her father, whose eye-sight began to fail more and more every day. She took care of him with filial tenderness and sought berries and herbs for his sustenance. Wandering through the forest, they arrived at a cave, into which Liba led her father, who had become quite blind. She prepared a couch of fresh moss for him.

Often, when she sat near him, the old man would take her head between his hands and kiss her hair tenderly and offer up a prayer.

He felt his guilt deeply, but he complained only for his daughter's sake whom he had, by his inconsiderate behaviour, rendered so unhappy.

One day they were sitting on the rock, enjoying the warm rays of the sun; the maid knelt before her father, whose hands played with her ringlets or caressed her soft cheeks, when suddenly the noise of steps was heard. Liba started and trembled, when she perceived behind the bushes the tall figure of a hunter.

„Schott!“ the maid wanted to cry, but the name died on her lips, for it seemed to her, as if the spirit of revenge approached in the person of her lover. A flood of tears gushed from her eyes and she began to pray, with hands uplifted to heaven:

„Oh God, if we have committed a sin, forgive us end our punishment!“

„Amen!“ added her old father, folding his hands fervently in prayer.

Just then a flash of lightning darted from a cloud and seemed to strike the rock; the thunder echoed hollowly through the mountains. Schott of Grünstein, who had seen the lightning and was anxious to see, where it fell, perceived with terror the corpses of his beloved and her father.

Seized by awe and respect for the decress of Providence he sunk down upon his knees and prayed.

The All-mighty had heard their prayer and delivered them from a painful life.

Schott of Grünstein buried the corpses on the place, where he met them and erected a chapel, on the altar of which was written the name of Liba. The rock, where the maid remained and took snch tender care of her father, received the name „Treuenfels".

Alten-Ahr.

On the river Ahr stand the ruins of a castle, of which the following tradition is related.

The last count of Alten-Ahr had two beautiful daughters, who were as lovely and affectionate, as noble and courageous; they cheered the old age of their father, who often said, he would sooner die, than lose his daughters.

One day two messengers entered the castle from opposite sides.

The old count received them and heard their messages. He read the letter with a troubled and anxious countenance. Then he repaired to the apartment of his daughters and delivered to each of them a letter. They read, blushed and looked at their father with a doubtful air.

„Well, my daughters", asked he, „what shall I reply to the messengers?"

„Can you ask?" exclaimed the elder one, „The daughter of the count of Alten-Ahr is too proud, to give her hand to a robber!"

„And you?" said the knight to his youngest.
She threw her arms round his neck, saying:
„Father, my answer is the same as Rosa's."

„I thank you, my children. These knights
are robbers. They will besiege us, but better
to die, than make an alliance with such fellows."

He tore the letters, delivered the pieces to
the messengers and bade them withdraw.

Some days after the same messengers delivered a declaration of war and a little later a
troop of soldiers approached and surrounded the
castle.

The count assembled his men, who were
experienced soldiers and entirely devoted to him;
he assembled them in the hall of his ancestors
and entered it, accompanied by his two daughters.

„Soldiers and friends!" said he, „the knights,
who are encamped before the castle, asked for
the hands of my daughters, who refused them.
Do you think, that they were right and do you
prefer death with us, than to surrender the castle
or will you leave us and join the enemy?"

„We prefer death", exclaimed the soldiers
unanimously.

„Then we will fight bravely and not surrender at any price!"

But the besiegers, who knew the strength
of the fortress, would not attak it, but resolved
to subdue the castle by famine.

Weeks passed and at last there were no more provisions.

The count assembled his soldiers again and addressed them:

„Friends, the provisions are exhausted and we have no other chance, than to risk a sally; if we don't suceeed, we must starve. I give you permission to leave the castle."

„No, no! We prefer death!" cried all.

„Well then, prepare for action!"

The sally failed. Those, who returned prepared with great resignation for death. Fever and famine raged in the castle and soon the old knight stood at the side of his daughter's corpses, surrounded by a few of his men. He put on his armour, descended to the stable, saddled his favourite steed, mounted it and rode in full gallop to the rampart of the castle.

„May our curses come upon you and I conquer you in death!"

Saying this he spurred his noble steed and leaping over the rampart, he plunged into the flood of the Ahr, which like a silver-string winds through the rich fields. Knight and steed perished. The enemy, who witnessed this heroic death, struck with awe and fear, fled.

The troops, who were sent to his succour, arrived too late. They broke open the gate and penetrated into the castle, where they saw nothing but corpses.

Seized by awe and grief at this horrid sight, they withdrew, for a reverence to the dead detained them from taking possession of a place, the inhabitants of which had died with such heroic resignation.

The castle was never inhabited again. It served only as tomb for the last descendants of the family of Alten-Ahr.

The two robbers, the authors of this crime, were vanquished and thrown into a dungeon, where they died. Their castles were demolished and their escutcheons destroyed.

Cologne.

e deeply regret, not knowing the name of that highly gifted man, who conceived the plan of that glorious and gigant structure, the cathedral of Cologne.

The following tradition gives an account of the architect of the dome, who had for many years been a gloomy and pensive man; his whole mind was absorbed by the reading of books and making plans on parchment.

The aim of all his efforts was to erect a magnificent building, but till now he had sought in vain to gather his ideas and to form a plan. All what he had found and imagined, could not satisfy him.

Tormented by impatience and as if in fever, he threw himself on his couch and soon the different plans which he had formed and rejected danced before his excited imagination and seemed to mock him. One plan only remained covered with an impenetrable veil and when the master tried to lift it, the parchment glided from his hands and an old idea, often rejected, met his eager eye.

Almost frantic the master followed the veiled image, which beckoned to him and led him to a rock, covered by the shadows of night. Then the veil dropped and with a shout of joy the master was about to seize the drawing but it suddenly disappeared.

With great anxiety and covered by a cold perspiration, the dreamer awoke. His heart throbbed, but his mind was quiet and clear and he was sure, that he had caught the wonderful plan, at which he aspired for so many years.

„Oh", exclaimed he with grief, why does the plan not appear again! O, that I might see it once more!"

He seemed to hear a noise in a remote corner of the apartment. A gray mist rose. Frightened and fearing mischief, the master wanted to rise, but a light laugh detained him and he saw Satan before him, with a mischievous, triumphant smile on his lips.

„Would you be content, if I showed you the picture once more?" said he laughing sardonically at the alarmed master, who exclaimed passionately:

„Let me see it and I will give you, what you demand."

„Oh, I demand very little! Only sign this paper and you shall have the plan!"

The architekt took it with trembling hesitation, for the letters glowed like fire, but when he read it. he started back, crying:

„Wretch! Away with thee! You demand two souls, mine and that of the first, who enters the church! Mine you may have, but another shall not perish through me!"

„Farewell then; you shall never discover the plan!"

The devil put the veiled parchement in his breast, at the same time lifting the veil a little so that the master could see a part of the plan. He stared with anxious and longing looks at the picture, and overpowered by ambition and curiosity the master seized the parchment, which he had rejected. „Stop! Don't take it! I give you my soul and even some years sooner, than you agreed."

„No, no! Signor, farewell!"

The devil pretended to go, but the architect detained him; the devil stopped, gave him the parchment and after he had signed it, he received the plan.

Many years had passed since that night and the construction of the cathedral was so far advanced, that it could receive the first consecration.

The architect was extolled by every one. The

archbishop received him at his court and the noblemen thought themselves honoured to be able to
converse with him. His name was on every lip
and his renown seemed as sure as the foundation
of his building.

He was indifferent to all praises and gloomy
and silent in all the festivities given to his honour and as the time of the consecration approached,
a deadly anxiety came over him and robbed him
of his sleep.

The citizens shook their heads and shrugged
their shoulders, when they saw him, running
through the streets, like a restless spectre.
Mysterious rumours spread about and when at
last they reached the archbishop's ears, he resolved
to question him on the subject.

The architect, who could no longer endure
the stings of his conscience, moved by the kind
words of the archbishop, revealed to him with
tearful eyes the mystery, which lay like a burden
on his heart.

When he had finished, the prelate knelt down
and prayed: the architect, who also tried to pray,
could not, violent sobs only issued from his breast
and died on his lips in forced laughter.

„You have grievously sinned“, said the archbishop, rising; „not only against your own soul,
but also against the salvation of annother. Go
home and implore the mercy of God. I also

shall pray for you and perhaps God will forgive
you and reveal to me, how we can avert the
evil."

Pale and distracted the master tottered home
and tried to do as the prelate bid him. But
it seemed to him, as if heaven were shut against
him and that the power of hell had made him
dumb. With a cry of despair he threw the prayer-
book into a corner, beat his breast and fore-head
and fell senseless on the ground.

The alarm of the citizens of Cologne can easily
be imagined, when they heard, that the first
person, who entered the cathedral, should become
a prey to the devil. They avoided with horror
the master's house and dared not even pronounce
his name. as if that would already put them in
connexion with Satan.

The finished part of the cathedral like all
the surrounding ground stood deserted and abandoned. The people spoke with sorrow of the
desecrated work and the archbishop bethought
himself of how the shadow which rested on it,
could be removed. It was at this time that an
ill renowned woman awaited her sentence in the
archbishop's prison. Scarce had she heard of his
perplexity and that of the citizens, than she offered
to be the first to enter the cathedral, on condition, that she should receive her freedom.

The offer of this notorious sinner was reported

to the archbishop, who after a long deliberation with his counsellors resolved to accept it.

On the day of consecration the whole clergy, the nobles and citizens, men, women and children flocked to the dome, to witness the strange spectacle.

After the multitude had waited impatiently for a long time, the gate of the archbishop's prison was opened and six men, who were scarcely able to stifle their laughter, appeared carrying a large covered box.

The bells tolled and the multitude, knowing, that the devil's victim was in the box, avoided it as much a possible.

At lenght the procession moved on. Behind the chest walked monks with holy water, who sprinkled it: then followed the choristers and priests and last of all the archbishop surrounded by the nobility and an immense crowd of people followed.

When the procession had arrived at the cathedral, the archbishop read a prayer, the last words of which were repeated by the clergy. After the prayer two men opened the church door, and keeping a little distance off, the chest was opened and a female crawled forth on hands and knees; no sooner had she entered the church, when she was seized upon by Satan, who with

20

a horrible noise broke her neck and then fled, uttering fearful yells.

The archbishop fell on his knees as well as the multitude. Satan instantly flew to the house of the architect, and fled with his soul to hell.

No sooner had Satan disappeared, than a female stepped out of the chest and entered the church, where she knelt down praying with uplifted eyes to heaven.

The archbishop, recognizing, that the exorcism had proved successful, entered the cathedral with Allelujahs and the people followed with shouts of joy.

The servants carried from the dome the carcass of a pig, enveloped in a woman's gown, which had been sacrificed to Satan. The poor architect was found sitting at his table, horribly disfigured and with his neck broken, the fatal plan before him and his prayer-book thrown in a corner.

He was buried privately. But the woman, who had cheated the devil, entered a convent, for the sight of the prince of hell had been a little too much for her conscience.

The lion-slayer.

t the town-hall of Cologne are to be seen two pictures, which remind us of the heroic deed of the burgomaster Gryn. The history of the Rhenish towns is one constant struggling of the citizens against the oppression of their spiritual despots.

One of those tyrants was Conrad of Hochstetten, a proud and ambitious priest, who in the year 1237 occupied the archiepiscopal see of Cologne after the assassination of Engelbert I. Conrad brought his despotism so far, that his citizens took arms against him under the command of Matthew of Overstolz.

Conrad marched with his troops against the rebels and was shamefully defeated. Still more inflamed against those, who had dared to brave him, he swore revenge, but was now more prudent; he tried to obtain by cunning, what he could not by force. He succeeded to set the citizens at variance and to seize the reins of the government.

His successor Engelbert II. followed in his foot-steps. He fortified his town still more and filled it with troops.

Now the citizens saw, that they had been shamefully cheated, but the military forces, which the archbishop displayed, intimidated them; although murmuring at his commands, they had to obey. But as the government of the archbishop became more and more tyrannical, Eberhard, a resolute, enterprizing man, summoned his fellow-citizens, to unite themselves and fight against the despot.

The burgomaster Gryn joined the noble Eberhard and like a fire-brand the desire of liberty inflamed every heart. The alarm-bell was rung and with its sounds mingled the clashing of arms and the war-cry of the citizens.

Cologne became a battle-field. The tyrant was vanquished and turned out of the town.

The furious prelate assembled an army and marched towards Cologne. He was obliged to negociate and recognize the rights of the citizens. Engelbert made his entrance at Cologne. He assembled the chiefs of the town and took them perfidiously prisoners in his palace, which was directly surrounded by his troops. At the same time his brother sent a considerable armed force to Cologne, but the citizens, being aware of it, rushed on them, broke open the gates of the palace and took the perfidious priest prisoner.

By the protection of a high person he was set at liberty but with the condition, that he never would molest the town again.

The archbishop never thought of keeping his word. On the contrary he reflected upon the means to triumph, like his predecessor by cunning and before all to render the valiant burgomaster powerless; for he knew, that he was the chief leader of the citizens.

For the purpose of getting rid of him, he thought of the following plan. He had a lion at his residence in Bonn, which was brought to Cologne. Two chaplains were to invite the burgomaster, to arrange a reconciliation.

The burgomaster was indeed surprised at the invitation of the two chaplains, but confiding in his good cause and the strenght of his arm he rejected the warnings of his friends and accepted the invitation. After dinner they showed him the curiosities of the palace. A door opened and when he had entered, it was shut immediately behind him with a scornful laughter.

Gryn, who recognized with indignation and horror the perfidious snare, which had been laid for him, was still more surprised, when he perceived a lion, which in all his majesty and ferocity regarded him with sparkling eyes and roared with hunger, lashing his tail from side to side.

Scarcely had the burgomaster time, to draw his sword, roll his left hand in his cloak, when the furious beast rushed at him. He had the presence of mind to thrust his left hand in the animal's jaws and with his right to run his sword in the lion's flank. This heroic deed was performed in a few minutes and the vanquisher of the lion sank instantly on his knees, thanking God in a fervent prayer for having rescued him from so great a danger.

He waited a long time to see, what would happen. The clashing of arms mingled with the furious tolling of the alarm-bell soon made him aware of a new disaster of the town and a little after his friends, accompanied by the two trempling chaplains entered the room, where the valiant burgomaster stood by the side of the dead beast.

A cry of revenge was heard throughout the town, when the shameful treason was known. The two chaplains were hanged and the burgomaster carried triumphantly to his house, where his wounds were healed. The citizens sent their complaints to the emperor. The archbishop accused the two chaplains and approved of the hanging of the two criminals.

To gain the favour of the common people
and render them jealous of the nobility succeeded
better. A civil war broke out, in which the
party of the archbishop under the command of
Weissen, count of Limburg and the kindred of
Engelbert was defeated.

The „Overstolzen“, the party of the nobles,
got a glorious victory, turned the strangers out
of the town and persuaded the citizens to join
again to their party.

For the purpose of increasing their power,
they made a defensive alliance with the counts
of Geldern, Julich, Berg and Katzenellenbogen,
who where also appointed arbiters between the
town and the archbishop.

Engelbert, whose fury increased after each
defeat, attacked the count and their towns,
especially Julich.

Now the confederate towns joined their forces
and attacked the prelate's army in the plains of
Zulpich and Lechnich, where the archbishop,
commanding his troops personally, was not only
vanquished, but taken prisoner. The count of
Julich carried his prisoner triumphantly to Cologne and then imprisoned him in the fortress
of Niedeck on the Ruhr, where he was obliged
for his humiliation and the pleasure of the people
to show himself publicly for some hours in a
cage of iron.

Later, by the intercession of the generous
Albertus magnus, who was first teacher at Cologne, then bishop of Regensburg, the count
granted him his liberty, but through grief and
shame he died a short time after his release.

———

The white horses.

t the time of the great pestilence, which raged through Germany in the year 1440, the beloved wife of Sir Aducht fell victim to the plague and was buried by her husband who deeply lamented her loss. The sextons, who had remarked with convetousness the rich ornaments, with which the old husband had adorned the corpse of his beloved, opened the tomb in the night and broke the coffin.

The deceased rose with a sigh, while the sextons deadly pale with terror fled. Recovering by degrees and recognizing, where she was, she cried for help, but nobody could hear her; she then stepped out of the coffin and tottered shivering towards her house.

It was late at night, when she arrived at her home on the „New market." She knocked repeatedly, till at last the husband opened the window and asked, what the matter was.

„It is your wife Richmodis, whom you believed dead. Oh, descend quickly, dear husband, for I am exhausted by cold and terror."

„You are a rascal, to put such a joke upon an afflicted widower.

„No, no, I am really your wife, I still live."

„That is as impossible, as my horses can come up-stairs."

At this moment he heard the trampling of his two horses on the staircase und when he looked down, he perceived the two horses standing at a window and looking down from it into the street.

In great haste, but not without some fear, he descended, opened the door and received his weak and shivering wife in his arms.

Both lived many years in perfect harmony. And in remembrance of this event, Sir Aducht ordered two horse's heads to be made and fastened on the front of the window, where they were to be seen for a long time afterwards.

Index.

www.ingramcontent.com/pod-product-compliance
Lightning Source LLC
Chambersburg PA
CBHW020936030726
47496CB00005B/1212